FORMED

FORMED

BOOK 1

MANGLED

JACOB E. SANDERSON

TATE PUBLISHING
AND ENTERPRISES, LLC

Published by Tate Publishing & Enterprises, LLC
127 E. Trade Center Terrace | Mustang, Oklahoma 73064 USA
1.888.361.9473 | www.tatepublishing.com

Tate Publishing is committed to excellence in the publishing industry. The company reflects the philosophy established by the founders, based on Psalm 68:11,
"The Lord gave the word and great was the company of those who published it."

Published in the United States of America

ISBN: 978-1-68333-371-5
Fiction / Christian / General
16.06.13

Contents

Preface

Is it possible for a child to reach adulthood without conflicting with the parental plan? Are parents' expectations for their children unrealistic? Could it be that parents don't anticipate the problems they will face? Is there a constructive backup plan for failed expectations?

The dilemma in targeting the correct philosophical perspective on parenting is perhaps without rectification. Is it even possible to be a successful parent? If so, in whose views? Opinions often appear to be more numerous than parents. Who actually holds the most successful ideologies? Is there a correct or incorrect method? Could the best solution be found in an ethnic culture or religious teaching? If so, which one? The Buddhist Four Noble Truths, the Book of Mormon, the Muslims' Koran, the Analects of Confucius, the Jewish Tanakh, an agnostic view, or the Christian Bible? If so, what version or by who's interpretation? Perhaps all there is to actually know, or comprehend, about parenting is only to be found in one's hindsight.

As a Christian, I am first compelled to gather insight from the Holy Scriptures. Whether it be through a minister, a counselor, a teacher, a friend, or from a mere paperback, the reference source absolutely must be in alignment with the teachings of the Bible. As a human being, I find that parenthood enhances the motivation to find the answers toward many of life's questions. As a student of life, along the way, I have developed many opinions of my own. The fact that I am not a world-renowned author, theologian, nor philosopher makes this writing and its message no less relevant, considering my reference source is the divine will of God. Therefore, judge not the orchestration of my words or the political correctness of my thoughts without first subjecting them to the test of truth in Scriptures. Reality and the truth alone will ultimately judge this book according to its practical uses and the extent of its effectiveness. I have found religious thoughts regarding parenting to be lacking some very basic rational skills. In fact, some religious beliefs and teachings grossly contribute to inadequate parenting skills.

Do not get defensive and follow the religious reflex that tells you to just quit reading this. Please bear with me. Accepting anything as a truth or reality is like believing by faith—it requires compelling evidence presented by a credible source. Therefore, I fully intend to provide no less for the attentive reader.

While this book series is designed with the intent of sending a resourceful message to educators and other professionals within the realm of Christianity, it also can speak volumes directly to the heart of every Christian parent and parent-to-be. It will also be of special interest to veterans and their families. In addition, it can be of a very special interest to those incarcerated and their families. It is to the lost as well as to the saved!

The complexity of this work achieving such a broad-based audience and maintaining clarity or a focused agenda may limit a full understanding of this work to the more avid readers or at least those with some patience toward grasping its content as a whole. Those capable of pondering collective thoughts without requiring it to be so line-by-line captivating. The storyline and testimonial itself is much more readable and reaches out to an even wider audience.

This story is intended to be thought-provoking, containing topics ranging from alcohol, drugs, sex, criminal activities, acts of war and street violence, which may be too mature or graphic for some readers. In addition, it also contains some demented biblical views, exposing some horrific incidents within some churches. While its purpose is to clarify the difference between right and wrong, some people can and will distort what they read to the point that this material could be as destructive as the

Bible is in their hands. Let this be clearly understood; any grievances implied toward a church or specific religious group in this book is to expose the evil at work, not to belittle or mark any Christian denomination. The same evil is very much alive in absolutely every church. Evil is the focal point in this saga, not a particular denomination.

Expect some of the material to be difficult to analyze without researching my findings. While some may classify this as a self-help book, its design is not intended to be. It is merely a combination of thoughts inspired or provoked by the story within, to then be a mere tool used to point to the book that can help—the Bible.

At a shallow glance, one may fall victim to an assumption that this book critically implies a troubled child is little more than a product of poor parenting, removing self-blame or responsibility. However, I assure you if you invest a deeper exploration, it exposes a focus on the root cause, which is not necessarily the parent. As history itself has provided, exceptionally well-behaved and good-natured children have been produced by bad parents. Likewise, poorly behaved children by what would otherwise be called good parents; thus, discrediting such an isolated accusation.

Educators of the faith hold the greatest responsibility to distinguish between good and evil in teachings and will ultimately be held to the most significant accountability.

As humans, however, we are inclined to hold all people accountable for their actions, as we justly should. However, during this accountability judgment, evil itself often escapes being credited with little, if any, portion of the blame. This is intensified when religious beliefs or opinions exceed biblical teachings. Also through a shallow look, some may think this book implies that troubled children are the result of religious thoughts. This also demands a closer look discerning between religious teachings and what the Bible actually teaches.

In the opinion of some, even the Bible itself does not justly exalt good parenting no more than it has eliminated bad parenting! This is because evil is ever present. Therefore, there is not, nor can there be, a quick or easy fix for bad parenting, or for every ill-mannered child. One certainly cannot spend an hour or two reading a book of any kind, especially the Bible, assuming you can then put it on a shelf and it will have provided the means to fix twenty or thirty years of corrupted issues. However, if your eyes are open and your heart hungry, and you search the Bible through a structured study, you can find so many notable uses for parents that no self-help book could ever compare, But the bottom line is as always: you can lead a horse to water, but you cannot make it drink. This book is intended to just corral more to the edge of the river with the hope of increasing the reader's thirst!

Introduction

The developmental process from child to adult should include an ordinary childhood, though perhaps not necessarily the "fairy tale" childhood that parents ideally would have. Nevertheless, broadly, parents generally agree the intended life hoped for a child will be one that would ultimately produce sweet dreams rather than nightmares and pleasant rather than depressing or dramatic memories.

Natural hardships and struggles of life commonly provide a variety of factors that contribute to the molding of a child. One's physical and/or mental structure from birth to the experiences they go through as a child. A death, such as the loss of one or both parents, grandparents, or a sibling, or a playmate is a typical life-altering factor. Eventually every older person experiences such. However, generally the younger the child and the closer they are to the deceased, the more the circumstances impacts one's life. The number, or frequency, of traumatizing incidents one also experiences contributes to the degree of change.

Geological, social, religious, and economic settings have a partnership with the parents in structuring the type of citizen, husband, wife, or parent the child will become. In our modern culture, the stability of the home itself is an ever-growing factor. Divorce has become so common that one may wonder if it is not the norm. It is not uncommon for children to have been parented by two, three, or more stepparents. Many children are also without parents at all; tossed to and fro within the foster system before adoption, or just remaining within the system.

In addition, the confusion now in defining parents as a female mom and a male dad is becoming increasingly perverted by the gay movement. Now with legalized same-sex marriages, while a force works to silence the church's voice for truth, the dilemmas have escalated way out of control. This promotes the "no means yes" mentality. Why? Many religious leaders would just say "same-sex marriage is against God's laws!" However, in a nutshell, when adults change wrong to right, or yes to no, they have removed the element of absolute truth. Therefore, there can be no absolute yes or no! Now more than ever before, children are starting out in a confused setting, giving them a far less chance of maturing as part of a functional Christian society.

There seems to be a blatant disregard for a focused plan for the best interest of the children. The faulty building materials we have been using for years has severely undermined the stability of our youth's foundational structures. A warped-thinking child then grows into adulthood to create molds of their own. The next generation adds its corrupted thinking to form the next mold. At some point, whatever the children's structure may potentially be, it will lack the ability to withstand the upcoming storms of life.

Another dilemma is our educational system. In low-income communities, this is dramatically worse. High school graduates seem to have become a minority or at least those with 3.0 or better averages, while the percentage of youth-related crime and teenage pregnancies becomes the majority. Social structures have tragically ignored all the warning signs, while promoting safe sex and even abortions without parental consent in place of teaching abstinence or biblical marriage and family values.

Society is increasingly accepting such things and their effects as a standard part of life. The church has a vital responsibility in the role of reaching out to surrounding communities, yet it seems to not be doing enough to even prevent such from becoming accepted in the church itself. This is responsible for creating more terribly sad victims of society.

Today, the church appears to be producing fewer discerning Christians. It is often taught that Christians are to be rooted and grounded in the Word, yet the self-sustaining biblical family has become an endangered species. This is primarily due to our having permitted deception to erode the stability of even our Christian leaders. The abnormalities this produces is so disturbing that every Christian should be in constant prayer over this. As a result, you may encounter individuals whose lives have been so dramatically altered or are indescribably shocking even by today's standards.

This book was inspired by a true story of just such a case. Some fictionalization was necessary to fill fragmented or partially known truths. In addition, exaggerating and downplaying some events deliberately was done to alter facts as an essential deterrent for the protection of true identities. In Proverbs 20:19 it could basically be interpreted to say; avoid the one who reveals things as a gossiper. In protecting identities, this work also then eliminates such finger-pointing as if to gossip. This also eliminates pointing fingers to the good deeds of some, removing the potential credit or praise, the pats on the back that creates big heads and prideful looks that demotes the Christian character of many.

Christians recognize Jesus Christ, as the Master Potter. However, this is conditional upon the willingness of the clay (mankind). Generally, humans have a mind of their own and, more often than not, are formed carnally more than spiritually. This is a story that exposes the process of forming the molds that the lives within are shaped by. From how the mold was formed that had shaped a man, to the mold-maker he then becomes. The story takes the reader on an unbelievable journey, to end by focusing on causes and preventions. In this, displaying a testimonial of transformation. Be mindful that a butterfly does not dote upon its days as a caterpillar.

This three-part saga is called *Formed!* It introduces you to the life of a man called George. In learning of his story, he told he had a bad childhood and had become a Christian at age eighteen. Quickly gripped by his strugglesome journey to make the changes he felt must be done, to learning just how difficult such changes were to achieve. To then learn his personal testimony was not wanted or welcome to an open-church congregation, beyond stating the basics that he once was lost and now he is found. Pastors and ministers who would get to know this man shared their wisdom as to why his story was not for everyone.

He appeared to be incapable of telling his story in an understandable or relatable way without the implications of wrongdoings of other people. It was full of, what appeared to be, battery toward multiple religions; in addition, it was full of adult topics. Although he came to understand this, the longing to share what the Lord had done for him grew. With the privacy and even the safety of his family and friends at stake, he began to share his story, and I started to creatively write leaving the actual identities untold.

Book 1 is *Mangled!* It is about the dysfunctional home and disturbed childhood of a boy named George. He is a near-illiterate, inner-city white boy in a predominantly black community, who grew up surrounded by the effects of war and domestic violence, who just happened to also suffer from ADHD. The story never focuses on his disorder as a cause or excuse for his situation, rather it is an outline of but one of the underlining conditions that manipulated, or neglected him. Along with the poor parenting skills, the professionals that dealt with him, to the peer pressure through sex, drugs, and alcohol as well as the violence he experienced through his youth. His childhood and his mind had been so mutilated that he was to start his adult life as a newly born-again Christian, maimed by his past.

Book 2 is *Entangled!* While this book primarily focuses on George's adult life, it exposes the lasting effects of his youth. In this era of time, he realizes that he is abusive and carries many old habits, and although he faces up to it early, the transformation process proves to be more than timely because he is so tangled up in, and easily snared by his past. With nothing restricting his disorder, he experiences some very compulsive behavior and acts out in some destructive ways. In this, he leaves a wide trail of consequences before he finally becomes capable of constructively instructing others. Books 1 and 2 are essential reads toward fully grasping Book 3.

Book 3 is *Intertwined!* This is more than a conclusion to this man's story, it provides preventative insights for future generations. It expresses compelling evidence supporting patterned links from the problems to the cause. Exposing how the past can get so twisted and woven into one's current life, that it can dictate the future. It also describes ways such a past can be a positive gift toward the future. Given this, a probable likelihood is projected toward a release from these apparent curses, or should I say learned behavior traits.

Many adults today can relate to or even resemble George and his struggles with the realization that few understand them because of the dark secrets buried deep within their minds. While this often leaves many feeling as isolated as the character in this story must have felt, people often overlook that one is never alone in his or her misery. People build walls around these things to hide within, then in their loneliness cry out, "I am so misunderstood!" Some words once spoken by the late Mother Teresa come to mind, "It is more important to understand, than to be understood."

Adults should keep pressing forward, encouraged by knowing from under what rock they crawled. In this, they should clearly see hope for others without the arrogant thinking that they are better than another, especially those of us holding Christian beliefs. This enables a literal understanding or personal experiences to be the practical means of offering hope. In turn, often giving evidence of a positive purpose to the difficult or tragic circumstances one has endured. See Romans 8:28.

Most trauma victims, if given the option, would like to think their ordeal could have been for some greater cause beyond just being a victim. Perhaps by using hope to make a difference for someone else is a good place to start. It has been repeatedly proven that one of the best natural forms of antidepressant is to focus on doing something good for or to others.

From a psychological standpoint, the leading character in this story, feeling remorse and responsibility for many things he caused, the release of his story then becomes a form of restitution. Through the hope that his story can accomplish some good through motivating more compassion and persuading the use of wisdom. Not out of guilt, or shame, for a self-therapeutic agenda, nor as some sort of confession to clear the conscience, but simply out of love. That is exactly what it will take to prevent such tragedies from being repeated in our future generations—love through understanding!

Regardless of how true or fictionalized you may consider this to be, it is about the story of a very real person. This is often about interactions with others and may only describe one side of the story. Therefore, in fairness, the reader should consider two-party situations from one party's perspective may only be partial truths. However, it is the arrangement of the many truths within that should be tallied. This is arranged to provide insight that could enlighten and alter the thinking of an abusive or neglecting parent, and help a victim or an adolescent with similar problems. The autobiographic portion of dialogue is merely a cover; the book's depth is about the journey of discovering causes and explanations and promoting wiser choices!

As a Christian parent myself, I found this story extremely awkward to write. The material is at times shocking, containing appalling incidents; however, this has stirred many productive and challenging thoughts. It is truly a disturbing story; however, much of its content is notably informative and can be applied toward prevention. While parts of this would never be described as heartwarming, it is certainly thought-provoking and heart-challenging. As it vividly describes many of the ways that destruction often appears to win, it clearly exposes the victories that one can have in battling life's struggles. Its message is one of encouragement that accomplishments are very obtainable through Christ.

All opinions and implied advice in this book are merely opinions and should not be substituted for or mistaken as professional instruction or counseling. This book and all of its contents should be subjected to the strictest scrutiny based on biblical principles before allowing anything contained within to alter one's own opinion. The book's design is to motivate the internal personal debate between good and bad with the goal to influence better choices.

There nearly always will be someone in a safety class that rather than learning safety, would make a paper wad from the instructions and would shoot it through a straw, but when someone gets shot in the eye with the paper wad, it's often said to be the instructor's fault. Understand this clearly: the Bible will certainly be misused and misunderstood. As with this and many other books; however, the reader is ultimately the one responsible for the actual decisions made.

But to those of us who promote their ideology or concepts using the Bible as a reference or source, it should not be without acknowledging that everything said will be recalled before God, where we will give an account for all. In this task, I sincerely pray my use of his Word will be correct, pleading with the reader to judge for themselves the origin of my views based only on biblical principles.

Note of Thanks to the Readers

A side from the above description, what this book series speaks loudest is that just because Christ died for you, He never does the work of living a Christian life for you, that's your job! Believing that all is to be forgotten once you're forgiven feeds deception, and if fed it can easily outgrow your Christian growth!

Being an author is much like being a cook; if you're a terrible cook even the hungry won't desire your food. However, even if you are a great cook people who aren't hungry will simply not want to eat your food. Thank you so much for investing the time to read this story. Doing so exposes your spiritual hunger and earnest desire for truth. I pray you find a savoring fulfillment in what I have cooked up toward stopping some of the deception for our future generations.

Sincerely with God's love,
Jacob E. Sanderson

1

The Mother's Side

There once was a boy named George. He was born into what on the surface seemed like an ordinary family. He had a mother, father, and siblings; they lived in a quaint little house in the city. He had aunts, uncles, cousins, and a grandma. George's mother and father both had jobs and were hard workers and were gone a lot. The children stayed with their grandmother while their mom and dad worked. Through his early years, George enjoyed playing with his siblings, cousins, and other neighborhood children. In this so far nothing in his life seemed abnormal on the surface, least of all to him.

The fact was, there were plenty of things wrong with little George's life. Although this story is primarily about him, we must first understand how he was formed. Let us begin by taking a closer look into what guides a boy into manhood—the mold. His parents were given the task of forming this mold. Although many factors contribute to what actually shapes one, it starts with the parents. His mother's name was Isabelle and his father's name was Otto. We will start by describing his mother.

Isabelle had grown up to be a real-life hillbilly. She would actually prefer opossum stew over a steak dinner at a fine restaurant, and nothing would replace a washboard and homemade lie soap. She was forty-one when she gave birth to George. But let's not start there, let's go back a bit further. She was born in a log cabin on September 26, 1917, and was raised in the backwoods of the bootheel of Missouri.

But let's continue going back a bit further, back to her roots. Her mother's name was Irene; she was born in late 1870s in the backwoods of Arkansas. Her father's name was Jack; he was born in the 1860s in the foothills of Kentucky. Isabelle's parents were very hard, dedicated workers and very devout Southern Baptists. Photographs indicate that they, like many of that day, generally appeared parched in character, with a sobering or serious look and seldom smiling, at least not for a photo.

They had very strict religious ideas for guiding their children. Her mother disciplined all the children, as well as teaching them to do many of the chores around the farm. The girls made and mended all the clothing and beddings, while keeping the large one-room log cabin clean, as well as the barn, chicken house, and the outhouse.

Girls of this time, within this culture, not only cooked but also cleaned much of the food. They skinned the rabbits and squirrels and plucked the feathers from the chickens; mainly all the small game.

The boys were included in some of this until they were about six or seven. Then they would begin to learn about the things that were considered to be boys' chores from their dad, such as gutting the hogs or dressing a deer. The boys eventually would get the more physically demanding tasks, but make no mistake, the girls would be required to work just as hard at whatever their job happened to be.

Each member of the family had duties, even her mom and dad. Her mom's (Irene) part was also to teach the Bible to all the children, as any good Southern Baptist woman of the time would; while her dad (Jack) would teach them to pray. This was quite common during this period within this culture and religion. The parts of the Bible she would frequently explain were regarding order; how children were to obey their parents. Then it was extended to the sexes: how a woman was to obey her man and nurture the home; while the man was to be the head of the home and the provider and protector of the household.

Isabelle's mom had been raised believing this was the way to be moral and true to God. She taught the generations of family traditions and values that had been passed on to her. Her dad, on the other hand, taught them that they could have a personal relationship with God, but they must first be reverent toward a mighty God. He taught them to fold their hands and to sit very still and quiet, lest God or their momma would strike them down. At early ages they all learned to pray from their dad, but as a result of their mom's teachings, most could quote the Lord's Prayer before they knew the alphabet.

Isabelle's dad was a carpenter and a logger. He and the older boys had built their house. It was a large log cabin with only one room downstairs and a surrounding open loft area for sleeping. It has been described to have been about 26' × 32', with a woodburning cookstove at one end and a fireplace at the other end. The loft wrapped three quarters around, leaving the end wall with the fireplace open. The girls were on one side, the boys on the other side, and their mom and dad had the end. There was no staircase, just two sturdy ladders, one on each side. There were two windows on the lower level with inside and outside shutters to help keep the cold out. There was one such upper window also; it was located in their parents' area.

There was, of course, no indoor water or plumbing, however, for the times in this area, it was considered quite nice. There was an outhouse some fifty or sixty feet from the front door, that was their restroom, and there was a freshwater spring at the foot of the hill about two hundred feet away. They had dug a cistern about twenty feet away from the cabin to catch rainwater and would draw it up with a bucket. Water was a valuable commodity outside the rainy season.

They had two barns; one was somewhat closer to the house and was the larger of the two. It had a toolshed attached to the side of it. In this barn, they stored hay and grain for livestock feed. It also had two stalls for the horse and one for milking the cow. The toolshed part was not only a place to store tools but also it was a small but well-equipped woodworking shop as well. The smaller barn was several feet farther from the house. It had livestock stalls for cows and a bull pen. They also kept some grain, straw, and hay in it.

Then they had a chicken house a few feet to the right of the toolshed and at times had about thirty chickens. The chickens would run free by day and would nest at night. To the left of the barn several feet away was the hog house; it had about ten stalls, but they seldom had ten adult hogs. Adjacent to the hog house was the pigpen, where the pigs and hogs could wallow in the mud and get a sun bath.

Over the years, this would become known as the old home place, providing the background settings for the many coming events. It sat on two sections of land, which is two square miles or 1,280 acres in the bootheel of Missouri. She was eight or nine before they had dug the cistern near the house. This part of Missouri had red clay or rock. The hills were mostly of rock and stone and didn't hold water; the clay was what held the water. Before this, they literally would go down the hill to fetch a pail of water.

Her dad's primary source for making money was making lumber or fence posts, ax handles, and cutting stave bolts. Much of this he did at a sawmill about eighteen miles from the homeplace, but the ax handles he and some of the older children made in his workshop in the barn. This was work when there was less to do at the sawmill, or when weather hindered the eighteen treacherous miles to the mill. If not snow, rain would have the creeks out of their banks making passage impossible for the wagon.

On several occasions, he was caught in a storm while he was away and would have to wait a few days to return home. There were no weather forecasters beyond merely watching the birds or other things. Often the older folks would say, "It's going to storm because I feel it in my bones."

Her dad was also quite the carpenter and would also do work for neighbors. However, these were not his only jobs. They were farmers and he had to deal with anything and everything that the rest of the family was not able to do. They had one workhorse, they raised chickens for meat and eggs and they raised hogs; often seven or eight and they had five cows and a bull. From them they had milk, made cheeses and butter. They had plenty of these and they would give to those who were in need or sell or trade it, often for fresh vegetables, linen cloth, or coal oil. They would raise three calves each year to slaughter for meat.

Her dad and the older children—girls included—did the hunting and fishing. This was often a solemn or quiet time, fun mostly, but quiet time. Any who shuffled about noisily were not likely to go the next time and would often get stuck cleaning the fish that others caught. He taught them that fish could hear, and the way to get a rabbit or a deer was by sitting very still while remaining silent. Any who could not grasp this were not going with him.

Most of the time, her dad was gone working, fishing, or hunting before the sun came up, not to return until dark or after. Actually, until Isabelle was big enough to be of help to him working, she did not recall spending much time with him except on Sundays when there was church. It was about five miles the opposite way from the sawmill; there were no creeks to cross, so rain or shine, cold or hot, the mind-set was they were going.

Isabelle could only remember four times that they all missed going to church on Sunday, and they were all due to weather. Once it was like a tornado; the other times were blizzard types of winter. Sure there were the occasions when one may be sick with a fever or something, but then only one other would stay with the sick one and the rest would still go to church. The wagon would be readied while the breakfast dishes were washed. Isabelle and her sisters would all take turns holding the reins and driving the wagon to church.

On Sundays, there was also family prayer time before supper. This was a time of holding hands with everyone. The children often rotated seats and Isabelle would like it best when sitting by her dad. While praying together before meals as a family and going to church was the standard thing, it always made Sunday's extra special. Generally, on other days most were tired from working and often some would even be still out working, but on Sundays they would all be at the table at the same time. Also, commonly, mealtimes were a quiet time, but not so on Sundays; talking and laughter was not only permitted but encouraged. It was a time to catch up on all that had happened the past week and to discuss the next week's plans.

When she was old enough, about thirteen, Isabelle started working at the sawmill with her dad. However, what she still liked best was going hunting and fishing with him and boy could she do both. She ended up a better shot than any of her brothers, and often out fished them as well.

She always felt that she had something extra special with her dad because he would compliment her shooting, and on many occasions, ask her to go hunting with one of her older brothers. None of her other sisters were ever given this chance.

Isabelle was next to the youngest of thirteen brothers and sisters. She actually had two other siblings that little would ever be spoken of. Her mother after carrying a child nearly full term, she had a stillborn child. In addition, she had an older brother who was killed in World War I in 1918, at just eighteen years old. He went to war just before her first birthday and was dead before that November. Little more was ever mentioned of either of these two children.

All her siblings as well as herself got in on not only the work but also the fun as well. The many enjoyable times often came in short spurts within their work. The work always started early and finished late, to gather around the supper table when possible. After they settled, they held hands and their dad would give thanks, leaving room in his prayer for one of the children to finish the prayer. A different child would finish the prayer the next evening and then the next. Sundays were different, her dad would not pray at suppertime. One of the seven oldest children would take turns with this, but they had to also leave room for one of the younger ones to finish up the prayer. This was the law that bound a family together back then.

As for the school in this area during this time era, schooling was thought to not be that beneficial. The children were not able to go except about one-third of the time. The school of the time did not pass or fail a student. If you went three years you were said to be in the third grade; this did not mean you could read or write at a third grade level.

The boys in this part of the country would seldom go past the third or fourth grade. Their primary study was math and the ability to write their name. Once a boy could add and subtract, write his name, and could work like a man, he was thought to be a man and ready for life, regardless of his age! The girls often were privileged to go somewhat farther in school, but to many folks of this culture it was thought to just be a waste of time above the essentials. Isabelle was considered very fortunate to have even gone to the fifth grade in her family. However, she never actually learned to read as well as the average second-grade student.

The schoolhouse? Why of course it was uphill both ways! The school was seven hilly country miles from the farm and when they went, they walked. There was no school bus, the "family car" was a wagon powered by "real" horsepower and his name was Buck. The wagon could seldom be used as transportation other than the one trip on Sunday morning to church.

You see, a wagon, or a horse, were considered valuable tools. The wagon was most always loaded down with wood or something, and old Buck (their horse), even if he would not have been too ornery to ride, was always needed to pull the wagon, the plow, or used to drag cut timbers. After all he was a workhorse, not a pet or toy.

Isabelle had endured the callous upbringing the backwoods commonly presented during this time. Even in good times this was an unimaginably hard life. This area's ground being mostly clay and rock meant growing food presented a lot of hard work for little results. Growing little more than weeds was often the result of hours and hours of calloused or blistered hands trying to grow vegetables.

The month after she turned twelve, the stock market crashed and the Great Depression became a very real-life-altering factor for everyone. This brought such a strain on the very best of people. She thought that if they had not lived on a farm, none of them may have survived the time. There was no work at the sawmill and no one had money to pay for her dad to work for them. He was frustrated a lot, but somehow they made it through.

On numerous occasions, her dad would have a really rough day. This would have everyone on edge anticipating trouble but not from her dad, from her mom. You see, her dad would take it out on her mom and in turn her mom would take it out on the children. No one saw it, but they all knew their dad would hit her when one of them did not get their chores done, or if one of the children had done something wrong, or had done a chore but not quite the way he had said for it to be done.

When the heat was on one of the children for something they did wrong, the only thing her dad would say is "clear out." Everyone knew what that meant. They were all to head to the barn and quietly wait. Their mom and dad would stay in the house and after a little while their mom would walk into the barn with tears in her eyes and their dad's belt in her hand. She would call out the name or names of the condemned, and the rest were to quietly and quickly return to the house.

She would whip them as if she was trying to kill them. She would not say a word, just hit and hit, after hit. Then if you were the one who just got it, you were to stay in the barn until you could compose yourself to appear that you were not hurt, even if that was not until the next morning. Even the older boys would stay in the barn for quite some time before returning to the house. This was a time when respect was demanded.

Isabelle's dad never hit the children, but the children never raised a hand toward their mother either or they somehow knew they would have dealt with him. Even though he had never hit any of them, they were all deathly afraid of him.

Jack, Isabelle's dad, died shortly before her sixteenth birthday in 1933. Her mother died just after her eighteenth birthday. Her mother's death would especially prove to be a devastating turn of events for the two children not married off yet. Although the Depression was thought to be over for many; in the backwoods areas, it was not because the jobs were very few, and money was just as tight. All Isabelle knew how to do was housework, farm work, or doing sawmill work or carpentry work.

At just barely eighteen years old, having only gone to the fifth grade, Isabelle was alone to fend for herself in the mid-1930s. All her older siblings had already moved all over the country and started families of their own. The old homeplace and all the property was now being seized by the government for back taxes. Her parent's health had slowly depleted over about a three-year span. During this time, a banknote covered some of the taxes using farm equipment and other furnishings as collateral. With her parents now gone, the government seized the property and the bank pretty much had taken everything else.

Her younger sister, Rebecca, was much too small to be on her own, so some neighbors took her in. This was considered an act of kindness. However, the man of this house had another motive that would not be known for a few years to come.

With Isabelle being of age, the people in this culture expected her to find her own way; this was how things were done back then. If you or yours makes the bed, you and yours were to sleep in that bed, good or bad. That is just the way it was. She was now on her own with all life as she had known now gone.

This of course did not mean people of this culture were not compassionate or caring Christian folks. It was simply just the way tradition was passed on. Oh sure, some helped her; she spent several days at this home, then at that one, but each time it was clarified that the help was temporary, that she needed to find her own way in life because the Lord God had laid her fate before her.

So off to find work she went and the employers of that time were not exactly equal-opportunity employers. She knew how to do a lot, but there was very little "man's work" to be found for a young woman in small towns. This struggle for survival forced her to go to a larger city.

By the time she had turned nineteen, still having the childlike innocence and a naive outlook that she was destined for success, because on her mother's deathbed, she told Isabelle God showed her she was going to do well. So with the guts of any man she headed out all alone for the big city of St. Louis, Missouri, in hope for a job. She did this under the warnings of others to watch out for the "colored" people, because they will "get you." At this point, she had never even seen a person of color.

Isabelle did find work, but only part time and the first three years were particularly hard and tried her faith. She first found work at the St. Louis Farmers Market. And with no place to stay, she spent the first few nights under an overpass.

There was an older black lady who was walking by and saw her coming from under the structure early one morning. She asked Isabelle why she was under there and Isabelle explained. The older woman told Isabelle her name was Ms. Sweetie, and told her to meet her at the market when it closed that day. She did, and Ms. Sweetie had Isabelle not only over for supper but also had her to sleep on the couch. She stayed with Ms. Sweetie for about a week.

Ms. Sweetie was a fine Christian woman, and she took Isabelle to church with her that Sunday. This was a memorable ordeal. Isabelle didn't know what to expect when she went into an all-black church. Keep in mind this was very much a segregated time when white people would beat another white person for associating with "coloreds" and the "colored" folks were no different about this toward their own. But Ms. Sweetie went straight up to the pulpit and repeatedly hit it with her walking stick and got the attention of everyone. She then said, "This child needs our help, and we're going to give what we can." They then took up a collection and some of the women gave her some clothes and some essential cooking items. Ms. Sweetie died not long after this, and one of her sisters brought Isabelle her iron skillet. She had told her sister that she wanted Isabelle to have it.

Then the news of Pearl Harbor, World War II, was underway for the United States. She knew that one of her brothers was at Pearl Harbor. He was in the navy. As she anxiously awaited word on him, remembering that she had a brother who was killed in WWI she was worried. Many men started leaving for the war and jobs quickly opened up. Just days after Pearl Harbor, she found a job in a factory as a seamstress. Factories began converting over to make things for the military, and she also sought part-time work at another factory. She later learned her brother was safe. He was not harmed because he was aboard the submarine the USS *Indianapolis* and it was not in Pearl Harbor during the attack by the Japanese.

In the early part of a cold November in 1942, she learns that one of her other brothers who was in the army had been killed in action in North Africa. Then she learns that the youngest of her brothers (John) had gone into the army also. In the summer of 1945, news came in that the USS *Indianapolis* had been torpedoed and sunk by a Japanese submarine. Before any word as to her brother's status came, rumors had it that many survived the ship's attack only to be eaten by sharks. Then one day one of her sisters called and confirmed her fear—her brother was dead. He was said to be among the first casualties when the ship was hit. She later found some comfort after knowing that the rumors of sharks were no rumors. *The poor souls*, she thought as she sighed that at least her brother never fell to that fate. This shark thing really stuck with her, she made praying for all our troops as well as the families of soldiers a daily routine.

War had struck home for her. She was not able to attend the funeral because she had to work. It also going to be in California and she simply couldn't afford the trip. Then word came that her brother John was hurt badly in the war and was in some hospital in England. She continues working long and hard hours through this time but still makes poor wages. So the part-time job became a second full-time job. Working seemed to be a way to absorb time away from worrying about her hurt brother as well as all our soldiers. These jobs would only last until about the middle of 1945, when the war was finally over.

With her jobs both now gone and having not managed to save much money, hard times and choices were at hand again. She had made some new friends at church; she insisted that she could not have made it through this time without them. She did the best she could do at blending in with big city life and stressful times of this era. It was some time before she found another job. She attributes her survival through this stage to her church family.

Then a change would take place. In early February 1947, Isabelle had gone on a date with a man whom she worked with. He had been so kind to her she thought he could be the one for her. But then he brutally beat and raped her. She was hospitalized for a while but after the physical wounds had healed she was left with the emotional scars of a rape victim.

As icing on the cake, so to speak, she then finds out that she had become pregnant. Then as if in shame, she withdrew herself from all social life, except the Sunday church service. Here she developed a deeper and more lasting relationship with her God. Her church family grew distant as it became apparent that she was pregnant. She could hear the whispering and felt the daggers and the dirty looks from others. Regardless, throughout her pregnancy she continued attending church faithfully.

Then, at thirty years old, in October 1947, she gave birth to a son and named him Marty. He was to become her life for the next several years. She spent her time working and going to church, and listening to all the do-gooder's judge her for having a son out of wedlock. Of course most did this in ignorance to the fact that she had been raped, or of the formed opinion that she in some way encouraged the deed. Nevertheless, this was a horrific slap in her face and she did not want her son to know that he was the result of rape. So she just would not talk about it and firmly took a stand against any who wanted to.

As time went, Marty grew and grew. Soon he was in school, then he was baptized. She was so proud of her son. Marty was a good son and a lot of help to his mom. He was a baseball fan and she would take him to the ball games. They developed a strong bond and neither would ever recall a single incident of problems with the other throughout these years. During the day, she worked and he went to school or to a sitter. On the weekends, they went to church and they had fun times doing things together.

This was through to the midfifties, and the Korean War then hit home also. One of her sister's oldest sons was killed. The funeral was to be in Kansas and her boss let her have a few days off. School was out, so the two of them took a train to see her sister and go to the funeral. The Korean War had not really been on her mind before this, but now she began to focus on praying for our troops again. She felt if something bad happened when you should have been praying but you didn't pray, it was partially your fault. She continued praying for our troops until well after the war was finally over.

It was now late July 1957, Isabelle found herself out of work again. The factory she had worked for was now closed down. During this period, her oldest sister from Indianapolis had written her a letter. Her husband had died, and she wanted Isabelle to come move in with her. Her sister had lived in Indiana for six years and had been going to a Southern Baptist Church since it started back in 1953. She had told her of a lot of jobs out that way, so she packed up and moved to Indianapolis.

Their time in St. Louis was an especially memorable one for Marty. Things that are no more, like Sportsman's Park and the St. Louis Browns. In addition, few things could impact a young baseball fan more than having an autographed ball handed to you from none other than Stan "the Man" Musial. It just couldn't get better than that for a St. Louis baseball fan. This now-Cardinal fan was moving to a state with no team, so it was going to be okay for him to stay a St. Louis fan.

Isabelle quickly found a job that paid ninety cents an hour. That was a fifteen-cent-an-hour increase compared to her last job. This was an exceptional amount back then considering that gasoline could easily be found for twenty-five cents a gallon, bread was often found at eleven or twelve cents a loaf. She had gone without many meals in the past to provide for her son and often felt despair. With excitement, she finally felt as if things were going to be better.

Then about two months after the move, without warning, her sister died of a heart attack. She and her husband had no children and now were both gone. What now? She thought, *I am alone out here to do it all again.* Her sister had been renting a house that Isabelle certainly could not afford so she was forced to find a place for her and Marty to live. Work itself was full of changes, and just having found a new church to attend and few friends, this was a lonely and nerve-shattering time.

She and Marty spent about a month living with one of the families from the church she had been attending. This gave her the time to find another place she could afford. It was an apartment in an all-white neighborhood; everything seemed to be segregated during this time. Their apartment wasn't too far from her job. It was within a block from a grocery store and a couple blocks from a Laundromat. The ladies from the church had a move-in party and provided her with some essentials. Among the things was a pull-behind shopping cart. This proved to be a treasured thing.

She used it to transport laundry and groceries. She would make one trip a week to the store and two trips a week to the Laundromat. Marty liked to pull the cart for his mom; it made him feel like he was a man. They had a confectionary next door to the Laundromat that had penny candy, and Isabelle would always have enough to get him a couple pieces of candy there.

She would often encounter other people at the Laundromat. There was one man in particular that she had seen there several times. He once offered Marty some change for candy, but Isabelle declined his offer. But then one day there were a couple of ladies in the Laundromat talking about Isabelle and referred to Marty as a bastard.

She then started thinking maybe she had come across "Mr. Right." His name was Otto and he did not like her child being called a bastard. He boldly put the gossiping ones in their place. As time went on she still was a bit standoffish toward Otto, but she began to think he could be the solution to her son being called a bastard. He acted like he could be a father figure for her now-ten-year-old son.

2

The Father's Side

Now let's take a closer look at the background of Otto, the future dad of George. He was born in Chicago, Illinois, on December 24, 1921. His parents were immigrants from Germany. They came to the States in the early 1900s as newlyweds. His dad was twenty-two years old and his mother was twenty years old. They came to the States along with some of his aunts and uncles on a big ship.

Let's first begin with Otto's father, his name was Georg. He grew up in Germany in a small community and had done very well through school. He was the son of a well-known leather worker who encouraged him to leave home to come to the United States with his new bride. Georg never learned to speak English very well; he remained too busy to ponder with such things as words. He was a hands-on worker; not that he wasn't a book-taught man he just never learned very much English. He was just an honest hardworking Catholic who had developed some valuable skills. He was exceptionally talented with leatherworks and people paid decent money for such quality work.

Georg was actually a shoemaker by trade, but his skills carried over into upholstering custom furnishings for the more prominent in the Chicago area. He indeed had done quite well for his family. They had a modest, but beautiful home that was nearly paid for, and he drove a 1922 Model T. But one morning in April of 1922, he failed to wake. At forty-one years old, his dad was dead. This was quite an unexpected death and his passing was devastating. This would prove to be life altering for all the family, especially for young Otto. He would miss out on all the things a son so desperately needed from a father, such as never hearing him say that he loved him. He could never recall an actual memory of him at all, only the passed-down stories.

Otto's mother's name was Ida. She was thought to be very wise and sought help in raising the children, of whom there were eleven total. She relied strongly upon the Catholic church and her sister, Maria, who up until now had been considering becoming a nun. Her sister now would move in with her and devote the next several years to giving her assistance toward raising the children.

The upcoming times were to be full of challenges for her as a single mother. Her late husband had accumulated somewhat over three thousand dollars, and although this was a lot of money in 1922, it was certainly not enough to raise the children on and live the rest of her life. They were going to have to make changes to assure their security.

She was smart enough to know that she had to look out for the future. She was a very educated woman who was particularly good with numbers. She was the daughter of a medical doctor and her mother was his nurse. She grew up surrounded by books and was inspired to read and learn. She was now longing ever so for her parents and other family, but they chose to stay in Germany. Her parents were killed around 1916 in an air raid during World War I. She had lost track of other family members in Germany.

Now just as her parents and other relatives made the choice to stay behind in a place they loved, she chooses to leave one that she has come to love. She sells the house and everything else that she felt was nonessential. They packed up everything else and moved to Indiana where her oldest son had now found a suitable job. There, they bought a much smaller and more humble house just large enough to make accommodations for them. It, of course, was in an all-white part of Indianapolis. She opened an account at the bank and deposited all the accumulated funds.

As time went on, some of the older boys also got jobs and gave half of what they made to her. Her sister had also gotten a job as a dental assistant and contributed. Ida took in some part-time bookkeeping for a couple different small businesses and they seemed to manage without touching their savings at all. In fact on several occasions they added more to it.

The early years of Otto were during the Great Depression; he was just about to turn eight when it hit. At this point in time, his mother Ida had accumulated some $6,200 from the sale of the other home combined with their prior savings along with what they had been adding to it. That was far above what the average single mother of eleven had.

Now the funds that they had worked so hard to keep were of little comfort. She being eager to watch out for their future followed advice to invest a great deal in stock. The bank that handled this for her was now closed, and no one seemed to have an answer. These were truly harder times than most had ever known. They had no idea as to where the next meal would come from, or if it would come.

The Depression did not stop most people from surviving; it did however enhance one's character. Those who banded together made it through with a greater love and appreciation for life. Those who made it by robbing and stealing from one another may have survived, but seldom recovered. Some would come to know God through this or grow closer to Him. The Depression naturally proved to enhance character, whatever it was. Unfortunately, Otto became inflamed with a more violently bitter and hardened heart toward God.

These truly were tough times, and Maria would now more than before prove to be invaluable to Ida. Both being very devout Catholics, everything they did in trying to raise the children was circled around the faith. For example, they were very big on making accomplishments within the church a more festive or celebrated event than others around them seemed to. These were such things as one's first communion or acceptance as an altar boy. This was such a big deal that it was considered to be far more important than a birthday, or when one begin to ride a bike, or when one hit their first home run. This was the issue of life itself to Otto's aunt and especially to his mother, even though the home run was important to others, such as it was to Otto.

They felt this would motivate all the children to do well, or better than they would do otherwise. Their philosophy was: this would do one of two things, it would either entice one to achieve more, or it would make one feel ashamed. Which they felt was a just reward for accomplishments or for the lack thereof. While their intentions were clearly of the best, and they certainly did not mean to condemn a lower achiever, this particularly had just such an effect on Otto. Throughout his childhood, he would recall no memory of having ever made them proud, pleased, or even content with him.

Otto was proving to be a troublesome one for having been raised in church and by such good and loving people. He was a good example of "the wayward son." He was unsuitable as an altar boy to say the least. You see, he carried a dark secret from his past; someone had molested him while he was still eight years old. Otto had been forcibly raped by his uncle. This was not just any uncle; this was his mother's brother, Hermann, who came to visit. He was a machinist by trade but he said the purpose of his visit was to talk to the family. He was thinking about quitting his job because he was considering becoming a priest. He was a much loved and respected man, friendly and fun-loving toward all. He was known as Hermann the German because he was so proud to be a German.

Otto had been sick with a fever one day, and it was time for mass. His uncle volunteered to sit with him while the others went to mass. Otto had been sleeping and was awakened by his uncle's forceful ways. Otto told his mother about what had happened, and she first assured him it was the fever talking, but over the next few days when he kept telling her she began punishing him for lying and insisted that he never speak of this again. His uncle never got the chance to become a priest. Instead, he was killed in some industrial accident a month or so later. This further enhanced his mom's attitude to not hear anymore about his slanderous remarks about her now-dead brother. But as for Otto, he was glad that pervert was dead.

He was so ashamed of what had happened that for over forty years, he would not talk about this incident. It became as if not wanting to be a homosexual somehow justified getting into fights to prove he was a man, most of which he started. Then this inner disturbance progressed. He began flirting with girls at a pretty early age, some in forceful ways. By ten he was experimenting with his nine-year-old sister Anna. By thirteen, she would become pregnant as a result of one of the many occasions he had raped her.

Being a rape victim himself, this further depleted his emotional state. Feeling his mom promoted this by calling him a liar; this was like an excuse. Regardless of causes, it was producing negative actions. Some psychologists may explain it merely as little more than an adolescent way of displaying or proving masculinity. Regardless of why such behavior now paved the roads to come with turmoil, not just for him but others as well.

Shortly before he turned fifteen, while still in need of a dad himself, he became a father; Anna gave birth to a boy. Being a dad however, would not be permitted. The child was quickly adopted out to an aunt and uncle a few miles away. They told both Otto and Anna that the child was adopted by a stranger in California. "It was for the best," they were both told. In addition to being told to never speak of this evil again. As time went on, more and more was to be bottled up. What more could be expected of him beyond having a rebellious attitude toward virtually every kind of authority.

Otto wanted to just take what he wanted, not become a slave to a boss or a job. Several tried to get him under control, but his rebellion ran deeper than any could reach. He was always getting into some kind of trouble in church, school, and with the law. He would do senseless things like the time he walked up to a newspaper stand and started a fire in the papers. Another time, he took a cab to the zoo, but had no money to pay the fair. He collected such a rap sheet of petty and juvenile things that when he finally did something more substantial the judge was not going to show him mercy. He then spent nearly the next three years in reform school for busting out a store window and grabbing a hat that was in the window. When he was released, he acted as if he had never went. His bottled anger seemed to be the driving force behind his mischief.

However, he just could not get a grip on his anger. So out of the boy's home for only a few months, now at eighteen, as an adult he is before yet another judge, and with a little persuasion from him, he joined the army. This was in a time when the military was quite frequently offered as an alternative to the jail workhouse for a year. He thought perhaps he might find something in the army that could change his way of life.

He enlisted for twelve months in August of 1940. This was the standard during peace time back then. This was just before President Roosevelt signed into law the Selective Training and Service Act of 1940. However, before his year was up, the US House of Representatives, by one vote, approved to extend a one-year enlistment by two more years. At this point, Otto was feeling like the government just gave him the shaft. He would have been out of jail for two years by the time they would get done with him.

Many of that day felt the same and there was a big rumor that many were going to desert when their year was up. Otto was in one of the barracks that had the letters O, H, I, and O painted on it. This stood for over the hill in October. Several did actually desert, so he wasn't the only soul with an attitude. But Otto didn't really think he had much to go home to anyway, so he stayed. Then on December 7, 1941, the Japanese attacked Pearl Harbor. Otto lost his brother, Friedrich, in that attack. And it was on! He wanted a piece of them Japanese, but the army had other plans for him. He was going to Africa and Europe and not to fight Japanese but the Germans—wait, Otto is of German descent.

He knew himself that his thinking was not altogether right and wondered if this experience was just going to send him over the edge. Emotional battle scars from wars and army life have twisted and mangled even the stable minded. He wondered what effects this would have if he were to even live through it.

He not only survived the war, and was highly decorated, but also stayed in the army for some time. He served from August of 1940 until June of 1955. He was in the First Infantry Division, "The Big Red One!" Among his medals were the Distinguished Service Cross, the Bronze Star, the WW II Victory Medal, the European-African-Middle Eastern Campaign Medal, the Army of Occupation WW II (Germany) Medal, and the Purple Heart.

His first taste of actual combat was in Operation Torch, the invasion of North Africa, the first American campaign against the Axis powers. In November of 1942, he underwent some additional training in England. A while later the First Division landed on the coast of Algeria near Oran. There were many casualties in the events that followed. It went from Algiers into Tunisia and by May of 1943, the German commander surrendered his forces and the Big Red One's work there was done.

Then they went on to help take Sicily in Operation Husky, going ashore at Gela, in the summer of 1943, and overtook the Italians. Then they faced nearly a hundred tanks of the Hermann Göring Tank Division. The navy helped with its gunfire and with assistance from Canadian allies, it was over the island's hills to drive the enemy back. Fighting continued until at last the First Division's work here was done and then they shipped out to the UK. He recalled that the battles in Italy had really been intense and very bloody. Very often they were assured of other Allied forces fighting with them in some of the same battles, but during the heat of battle you only felt the presence of the ones in the trenches with you.

On D-day, June 6, 1944, they went ashore at Omaha Beach. The beach quickly became like a junkyard of destroyed equipment. The dead and wounded blanketed the beach. It would appear there was little room for more to land, but somehow they did.

During the landing, the smoke from burning equipment and the dust from flying debris kept visibility low and the air hard to breathe. The shattering explosions were so vast and closely timed that the sound was more like a constant deafening roar. The noise was only good for one thing: it covered the sound of the many screams of those who had been shot or hit by debris, or shrapnel; many with their limbs blown off on the beach.

After the beach was finally taken, these men fought forward and liberated Liege and then through Belgium. At just twenty-two years old, with two stripes upon his shoulders, he was sickened by the brutality of war, seeing so many who were still teenagers wounded or dead. He did no more than they all did, and that was simply to press on, giving their all.

The First Infantry Division attacked the first major German city of Aachen and in October of 1944, the German commander surrendered the city. Their celebratory spirit could not exist without the reality that their victories were lined with the memories of their fallen buddies. By this point nearly one-third of them were wounded or dead. Reinforcements were no longer viewed as a sign of relief. It was more felt that it only meant more would die.

They continued fighting deeper into Germany, crossing the Rhine River in December. This put Otto in the Battle of the Bulge for that Christmas. The Big Red One held the primary shoulder of the Bulge. In January 1945, the First Infantry attacked and penetrated the Siegfried Line and occupied the Remagen bridgehead. They continually fought their way through 150 miles of some of the most brutal battles and terrain ever fought; much of this quest on foot to the east of Siegen.

They eventually made it across the Weser River into Czechoslovakia, and by May 1945, the war was finally over. This was as if it was a lifelong ordeal and the fighting was no more. The fighting first lived up to its motto: no mission too difficult, no sacrifice too great, duty first!" The major battles they took part in were: Operation Torch, Operation Husky, D-day, Battle of Hürtgen Forest, and the Battle of the Bulge. Some may think only the major or famous battles were tough, or that the First Division stood out above the others, implying they had more bravery than another division. Otto would quickly refer to any such thoughts as just stupid.

There were in fact many seemingly less significant battles that the intensity was just as great and his comrades were just as dead. In one such fight, his unit was pinned down, his companies' wounded captain was carried into his foxhole by a private who had been lost from his unit. Then a grenade followed and that private jumped upon the grenade. As a result, Otto, as well as five others, were saved by that soldier's sacrifice. The soldier who gave his life was no more than eighteen or nineteen years old. He was black and until now Otto had never touched a black person. But from that moment on, he knew the color was only skin-deep; we all bleed the same color. This was not a boy, he was not a negro, he was a United States GI who earned the respect of Otto. He then salutes his remains as if he were the president himself.

So let's get this right: freedom comes with a price and you didn't have to be someone special or belong to a certain group or to have been part of a particular battle to contribute. Otto would recall many other similar acts of true heroics, by even some who lied about their age, at just seventeen to the many nineteen-year-olds. Many of which gave their lives within the first moments of their first engagement with the enemy. Why? So freedom could reign!

Before it was safe to leave this foxhole, all but Otto and his wounded captain had been killed. His captain then tells Otto he would put in a good word for his heroics in saving his life. He didn't want anyone to know he was saved by a black GI. Otto quickly puts a knife in the chest of his captain and finishes him off. He later tells of the black GI's heroics to his superiors, but he never felt the young GI's family would ever be told of his bravery because of the prejudice of some. As for his dead captain, he was as proud of his actions in this as if he had killed Hitler himself. But no one had known what he done to him. This incident went into a growing collection of secret memories that would go untold for years.

By this time, all but three of the buddies he had originally landed in Europe with were either misplaced, wounded, or dead. In the heat of battle, you really didn't care if you got lost from your section, or squad, and ended up with another or if you ended up with a different company or even battalion for that matter. You didn't care if the one next to you was a different nationality or from a different country as long as his gun was pointed toward the enemy. He had fought with some French, with some Italians, some British, and with some Canadians; and he had killed and seen a lot of dead Germans, and said their blood was the same color as that black soldier's was. At least this was Otto's view.

As for the First Division, the historical facts include that some groups were virtually wiped out and others suffered fewer casualties. By the end of World War II, the First Division actually had suffered nearly twenty thousand casualties. Through the course of the war just over 43,000 men was all that had served in the First Division.

This group of men was issued 20,752 medals and awards, which included sixteen Congressional Medals of Honor. This spoke a very loud and clear message about the character of these men. Not that they were a single bit more significant, better, braver, or luckier than any other group of any of the Allied forces, or about any other battles in the war, but just to describe a clear picture of the men he personally served with and why he would have been so proud to have served with them.

After the war, some of the First Division remained in Germany as occupation troops until 1955. It was during this time period Otto got to see much more of Europe and learned more about his German heritage. There is no doubt that Otto served the United States of America and there is no question why he would feel like celebrating. He had every right to hold his head high and he should have felt as proud as he did to be an American. He had served, fought, and bled with the mighty First Division, and he would say that just by chance he survived it! But looking at the whole picture we certainly cannot just tip our hats to the First Division. There were over 16,000,000 Americans who served during WWII. The First Division was but a tiny portion of this number. In addition, let's not forget to give recognition to the other countries that joined the Allied forces, and their countless sacrifices. Be it known, the Americans did not win this war alone!

During his continued stay in Germany, there was much to do. For a long while, many GIs were about corralling the many prisoners who were taken in combat. They had to sort through them to see if some were responsible for war crimes.

The evil Nazi regime cowardly hid within the population as well as captured soldiers in an attempt to escape prosecution for their crimes against humanity. Many were sent stateside or to Britain for what was called a reeducation program. The Russians had taken a colossal number of German prisoners and it was rumored that better than half of them were murdered by the Russians; true or not, who could tell? What was very true, however, was the overwhelming bitterness toward the evil that had devastated the world; and the people responsible just happened to be German.

Many were held in General Eisenhower's special German DEF camps. Otto felt, as did many others, that General Eisenhower had a profound hatred for the German people, perhaps even comparable to the hatred Hitler himself had toward the Jews. It was said that he felt the more that died the better. He personally witnessed some very horrific acts of aggression toward the German people from individuals of virtually every Allied force. He also saw many great and courageous acts of compassion toward them.

In this era, he posed many questions in his mind as to why he was sent to fight the Germans and not the Japanese. Do not forget, although Otto was born in the USA and was proud to be and to serve as an American, he was German by descent. This was ground that his ancestors had walked on. He was haunted by the possibility that some of those he killed possibly were his own blood relatives.

Otto known of GIs sharing rations with German prisoners and then being threatened with imprisonment. Otto himself had been ordered to not feed or provide any shelter for some prisoners and if they were sick or wounded not to let the medics help them. True or not, one thing was for sure, there were an awful lot of German prisoners and they needed to be sorted and moved. This was a big job and one that Otto didn't like.

However, this sorting task seemed less important at first because there was also the gruesome task of what to do with the thousands and thousands of dead. The stench alone was demanding priority. They would dig mass graves and throw the decaying bodies in by hand and bulldoze them over. The odor from such carnage was utterly indescribable.

In some areas, it was so bad that they just dug huge holes and pushed the bodies into the hole with the dozer and piled more dirt and debris on top. One of these times Otto found himself driving a bulldozer because the driver just couldn't take it anymore. He went through two of the German prison camps. He knew the war had accomplished a righteous thing in ridding the world of Hitler and his evil ways. He claimed for many years to come that he could still see the boney faces of the many children who were starved to death that he buried. Only one word described Hitler to him—evil!

During the war, he had been shot in the leg once and was hit in the shoulder by shrapnel. Both times he returned to duty after treatment. His greatest casualty was the damage to his mind. It was scarred by the cluttered body parts of his buddies, some who had saved his life with theirs. This was combined with seeing firsthand the unspeakable atrocities the Nazis had inflicted.

It would be too presumptuous for anyone to think that any one man played such a crucial part in every one of these battles as to single one out apart from the rest. I also believe that it would be foolish to not consider each and every one of them as having played such a vital part in the war and just downright disrespectful to not give recognition to all those who served in but just one such battle of World War II.

These GIs were faced with circumstances that we can only pretend to imagine. They had two powerful forces fighting on their side: righteousness and each other. This was pretty much a unified understanding in the heat of battle. In the trenches you had righteousness, your buddies, and nothing else! Those who lived told that those who died, died believing that! All life as this country would come to know would not have been possible had it not been for such men.

He served and continued to live with the belief that the USA and its flag was the greatest on earth, but its leaders sucked! He believed that this country was worth fighting for, not its leaders. And a man who would not fight for this country regardless of its leaders was not worth anything.

He carried many scars from those years and his thinking was very warped and twisted. At one point, his intention was to make the army his lifelong career, but the chip on his shoulder was just too big. By this time, the Korean War had come and gone in spite of his wanting to be part of it. His orders were to stay put, but his mouth nearly cost him a discharge then. But his attitude just kept growing until his rebellious nature would no longer conform to higher authority in a peacetime era. He got busted back to private first class, after having been a corporal. The army had no use for him and his attitude anyway and he was glad to be out from under its politics. He was nearly given a dishonorable discharge, but somehow escaped this disgrace and was granted an honorable one, but only as a private first class, after having served for fifteen years.

So much has been said regarding his military background. However, it is all very crucial information toward understanding Otto and the mold he would form. After his discharge, he wandered aimlessly for several years lost in the bottle. It was never determined or ever told when he actually become dependent on the bottle; perhaps he was a drinking man throughout, possibly even from before the war, it is just unknown.

One thing is for sure; by the time he returned to the States he was an alcoholic. He would frequently look into the bottle and say, "I did my share of killing and digging pits and throwing bodies into them for a grave, and some gratitude the stinking government has to not want me." He was clearly damaged goods with no hope in sight. He bitterly hated anything about the government; he would have nothing to do with it, he wouldn't even vote. Many in that day would say that he had suffered shell shock from the war and simply never recovered. Shell shock in 1980 would become known as posttraumatic stress disorder (PTSD). He, like many of that day commonly did, just looked to the bottle for resolve.

He hated the public schools, the police, the IRS, and politicians of any sort. Yet he spoke of the USA as hallowed ground, like heaven itself and of Old Glory as the most beautiful of all flags. He believed the red stripes were to honor those who bled defending this great ground, the white was their righteous cause, the blue with the stars was in fact this good old USA under God's heaven. He felt the government lied to him and stole his life from him. As a result, he had a saying that he fashioned his life by. He said, "Nothing is worse than a liar and a thief, and I hate liars and thieves more than anything." And in that aspect, he would go on to model his integrity based on honesty. He would always be described as a very honest man by all who knew him. Yet he wouldn't vote to change anything he claimed was so bad. He was truly a mess!

He just couldn't agree with how they had busted him down in rank and told him to quit the army, when he had given so much of his life for this country. He would often refer to how General MacArthur disagreed with President Truman and said his policies were soft on the communists, and as a result he was fired, yet still remained a hero with stars. A chip was on his shoulders for sure, he felt betrayed by the US government.

That was until late 1957, around the age of thirty-seven, when Otto met Ms. Right, Isabelle. They met initially at the local Laundromat; however, one of Otto's sisters worked with Isabelle. Otto had just recently come to back to the city to get a job. He was staying with his sister Anna. Anna had invited Isabelle to bring Marty over for dinner and what a coincidence, her brother happened to be the man from the Laundromat. The relationship seemed to really take off when Otto found out that Isabelle had Marty due to rape, his interest was attached like glue.

At this point in his life, he not only regretted what he had done to his younger sister but also felt sorry for other like victims. Remember his sister had given birth to his son and he was immediately adopted out. While he was in the army, the folks who had him had died, and she was very briefly reunited with her son. But then Anna wrote him a letter explaining that his son was killed in a car accident at just seventeen. She would never again speak of the incident or of her son again, but seemed to be okay with Otto now. Also, for so long, Otto wished he had known his own dad and had been hoping to someday have another son.

So a rather short courtship began but for some reason unknown; his drinking problem was not a problem. Isabelle would soon begin being questioned why his drinking didn't matter before they were married. She acknowledged that she knew he drank, but claimed she didn't know he was an alcoholic. Perhaps she thought she could change that, or stop his drinking. Some speculation has to go toward the military link between them. Perhaps somehow attracted through her compassion and many prayers she had for the soldiers, or by her having lost a brother in WWI and two brothers in WWII and having another turned deaf through it. Perhaps it was that Otto and one of her brothers had been in the same unit in Africa where he died. But in truth, it was simply unknown.

3

Family Life

Regardless of the missing answer as to why the booze didn't matter, she was swept off her feet and stricken by love and him likewise. They were very happily married on Valentine's Day of 1958. He was thirty-six and she was forty years old. They moved into a small house in another community. It was a poverty-stricken area made up of diverse nationalities with the majorities being African American as the largest, and Hispanic second; leaving only about 25 percent white. This posed no issues with either of them because they were not prejudiced, and this particular area had adapted to desegregation without much racial tension of any kind.

Before this move, the school district Isabelle's son Marty had went to was segregated, and he would continue being bussed to that school for the rest of that year. Besides the church they went to was of mixed races, so adapting to this change was not mentioned to have ever been an issue. Otto's mother and sister lived just a few blocks away from them, and one of his other sisters and her husband and children lived just a few blocks further in the same community. Everyone worked and got along with each other pretty good for several months with no notable incidents.

Then in October of that year, Pope Pius XII died. This pope was regarded by even many of the Protestants as a light from God—a true man of peace. His strength was most visible in how he was a compassionate defender and protector of victims of war, especially of those who suffered the genocide that had swept through Europe. Now came Pope John XXIII and many Protestants were somehow distraught that his becoming pope was being so glamorously celebrated, he was lifted up as if he were God. And with Isabelle being a Southern Baptist she reflected some of those feelings and opinions. As a result some defensive tensions started rising against her, from Otto's side of the family.

Then just under a year after they were married, on one cold January morning along came George. Out of respect, he was named after his grandfather Georg, except they added an "e" to the end. It was now going to be good-bye to his "ghost" army buddies and hello workforce. From a barroom brawler to a baby-burping stroller-pusher he was to become, at least so Isabelle thought.

Soon afterward, grandma insisted on having little baby George baptized in the Catholic church. This would become the last known time Otto would ever go to a Catholic church service. Her sister Anna was chosen as a godparent. Isabelle was told she could only watch from afar, she could not even stand in as a Christian witness because she herself had not been baptized in the Catholic church. She, of course, then had her pastor have a dedication service for him in the Baptist church. None of her Catholic in-laws would even come, and neither would Otto. But they didn't say too much to her about this at the time.

Isabelle and Otto were very proud! Consumed with pride, Otto had to show off his prized son at the bar. This would prove to not work out too well. The first problem to come up was the booze. In this house, the Baptist defined drinking as a sin, while the Catholic view was that it was not a sin to drink. Isabelle thought she had won this argument for the first couple months after George was born. However, about the time George began to sit up and crawl around, he started insisting on taking the baby to the bar, and she got red in the face mad at him and told him the child was not going to any bar. Otto smacked Isabelle and told her to just keep her mouth shut, and she could go or stay at home but he was taking the boy with him. This went on for some time and each time she tried to give her input, he would hit her harder, and more. He would let her go too, but she was not going to stop him from taking the baby. Isabelle then would go along to assure George would be okay.

Then there was the makeup time for him hitting her. She would take Marty and baby George to his mom right down the street; she would leave them for a while when it would be makeup time. Yes, there was a lot of making up. He was always very sorry and would promise it would never happen again. He would on occasion throw some beer in the trash and tell her, "See, I quit!" Then often after they made up, so to speak, he would go pull them out of the trash.

Then on George's first birthday, Isabelle had baked a cake and had it all decorated up. She had gone to the store and purchased some ice cream, a few decorations, and a candle for his cake. She had prepared an excellent supper and had the table all fixed up for when Otto came home to eat before they were to have the cake. When Otto came back he was raging mad because she spent money on ice cream and stuff. He said the boy was too little to remember birthdays so it was stupid to spend hard-earned money on such. She had only began to express that she worked too, when he slapped her, and threw the cake, the ice cream, and the decorations into the trash. The truth was that he had lost most of his money gambling that week and he realized the rent was due.

Marty, her first son, tried to be a man and face off with Otto, but Otto just laughed at him. He picked him up and held him upside down and let him know he was the boss. He said he could drive his head into the floor and break his "blinking" neck. Then with a smile complimented Marty and told him his attitude was that of a man and he respected that. However, he was not quite ready to be a man yet, but he promised that he would teach him how to become one. Isabelle was deathly afraid Otto would kill him and she told Marty to never try anything like that again.

Her pastor had been telling her things like: Otto was going to hell if he did not change and that she was trapped in a bad marriage that would only get worse unless he got saved. Or if he did not get saved, the baby would grow up to be like him and topped it off with things like it was up to her to witness to him; making it her responsibility to get her husband saved.

When she would tell her pastor about him insisting she go to the bar, it was as if her preacher became spineless. The exact same man who was telling her that this man was going to hell for being a drunk then tells her she married him and she still needed to be submissive to him. If that meant going to the bars; she would just have to bear that burden. Isabelle had asked him if he would speak to her husband. Not only would he not talk to him but also told her he would not advise her any further about her situation. She absolutely had no idea as what to do, but she continued her quest to get him saved. Otherwise he was surely not only headed for hell but also would take little George with him!

This was not exactly constructive. Actually more often than not, it fueled his anger to a raging boil. Regardless of the consequences, she was persistent and just would not give up on his lost soul. She had become obsessed with getting him saved. She tried anything and everything she could think of, but nothing seemed to have a positive affect. She had talked to his mom, to his sister, to one of his brothers, to her pastor, even to her mother-in-law's priest; no one could give her advice that was of any positive use. The Catholic theology understood by everyone in his family was that he was saved; he was born and baptized a Catholic. By their thinking it was poor Isabelle who needed to be converted.

Somewhere during this time, John F. Kennedy was elected as president. Catholics all were for him and pretty much all the Protestants were against him. The

Catholics felt he was somehow going to advance the church, while the Protestants feared he would have to take orders from the pope. This again stirred up tensions in their marriage and with his Catholic family versus Isabelle. She was beginning to wonder if she shouldn't just keep her mouth shut and let them all just go to hell. But her conscience, or her insanity, drove her to speak her mind anyway.

Just over two years after George, came a little brother whom they named Fred, after Otto's brother Friedrich who had died at Pearl Harbor. The problem now with two screaming kids in the house, a hangover, and an unhappy wife, Otto was staying drunk most of the time. When he was not, he was slipping the boys some beer to help them sleep, so he could. He would continually try coaxing Isabelle to drink but she was so convinced that she would go to hell if she did, she would rather let him beat her to death first.

Somewhere in the midst of this era, the Bay of Pigs Invasion into Cuba takes place, and like a light switch goes on. Otto is at war again, and his nights exposed a horrified side that he would not speak of. For some time, it would just be war stories from his days in the army, as though they were the good old days, or he was focused on the radio for the latest news about what was going on in Cuba.

Then shortly after Fred began crawling, Otto lost his job, again. His boss kept smelling the booze and had been warning him. This was a very trying time for Isabelle, but fortunately the economy during this time was worker friendly with an abundance of jobs available. It was but a week or so and he was working again. This was already his sixth job since they were married.

He really was a hard worker when he was sober and had a lot of valuable experience, but the bottle just kept getting in the way. Again, Isabelle would try to get him to understand he was going to go to hell for drinking and again he would cuss her out or just start slapping her. On occasion, she would try to hit back or simply try blocking and this always proved to definitely be a no-no! Once, it cost her eight stitches under her lip. Of course, she said she had fallen from a stepladder.

As time goes on, the drama unfolds as layered blankets covering all sanity. Now with George three years old, Isabelle is finding she just cannot win against Otto's drinking. She did not want the kids or herself to go to the bars, yet she felt helplessly trapped. Otto just kept forcing her to go with him and his abusive ways were quite sufficient toward controlling her. He would frequently spank her as a child with his belt, except very brutally, leaving welts and bruises. Besides, his brother, his wife and children, and one of his sisters and her husband and children would also go. The women did not drink, so it was the most tolerable of her options.

The Protestant and Catholic beliefs generally had very significant differences, but to this couple, the differences were like life and death. What he called good, she called bad. Her yes was his no, and vice versa. Why this did not make a difference before marriage the children would never know. However, this was but one of many upcoming notable incompatibility factors. Otto's life had been consumed by the military, war, and the bottle. The bottle was the thing they just couldn't find common ground on. The military topics were however, something they were both drawn to and perhaps it was this tie that had kept them together this long. It was around this time that the movie, *The Longest Day*, was at the theater.

Otto insisted Isabelle go watch it with him, and she did. He went on for days and days telling how this part of the movie was right and that part was so wrong. But most frightening was when he was asleep. For about a month after seeing this film, he would break out in a heavy sweat, grumbling, and even screaming in his sleep. Isabelle would try holding his hand to calm an obvious nightmare to only have him arise with his hands tightly griping her throat. He would quickly calm and say he was sorry, but she was absolutely scared by this type of action on numerous occasions. But at the same time, it was also such incidents that compelled her to cling to him all the more. She felt compassion, trying to have understanding in this, knowing he had suffered some great thing that he would not speak of. She honestly felt he needed her, and she would be his only chance for heaven.

Unfortunately, her understanding was often viewed as intolerance; being void of compassion. When Otto was intoxicated he wanted to tell a select few of the blood and gut war stories, over and over, again and again of the Allied victory. He would go on and on talking about all the ladies in France and telling all sorts of dirty jokes. His language and his songs were so vulgar it was often so intolerable to Isabelle that she would build with pressure until finally she would explode and tell him to shut up. This was always when he would hurt her the most. Otto wasn't the only man in that neighborhood who had a mean streak; it would appear that most the guys would get plastered, get vulgar, and would go home and likely beat the wife and/or the kids if everything didn't go their way.

It would often seem her life was a little different from many others around them. If the women did not want to drink they were not forced too, but many eventually did, as if just saying what the heck. Drinking itself was not even said to be a sin in the Catholic faith. Actually the drunkenness or alcoholism was never recalled to have been spoken against even once through the particular church they went to. The times, the environment, the whole scene was a fertilizer for growing destruction.

The focal point of conversation at the local Veterans of Foreign Wars (VFW) Hall, or the American Legion, or for that matter even at an event at the Catholic-owned Knights of Columbus bar during this time was more likely to be on the Cuban missile crisis than on family life. A toast to your old and long-dead comrades at the bar was more likely than giving thanks at the family dinner table. Godly peace and wisdom were void at these bars, where many good Catholics would frequently gather more religiously than they went to church.

The normal routine was to religiously get plastered on Friday night, attend Saturday mass, get plastered again Saturday night, be too hung over to even go to Church on Sunday, but manage to get drunk again Sunday afternoon, and periodically go to confession to ask the also likely hung over priest for forgiveness for failing to make it to church on Sundays. As time goes on, such ignorance would just progress and so would the abusive behavior.

Once about the time George turned four, he would not stop crying after he had gotten a spanking, Otto told him to shut up, and he screamed louder. So Otto smacked him in the mouth and he lost three of his front baby teeth. It cut his lip pretty badly and they took him to the hospital to get stitched up. They said he was climbing up on the kitchen counter and fell off. The doctors never ask little George; perhaps he would have been too scared to say it was his daddy anyway.

Then when little Fred was only two, he was crying and did not quit when Otto told him to stop. Otto slapped him on the side of the head so hard that it literally busted Fred's eardrum. Fred was in the hospital for a couple of days. Otto told the doctor that he had fallen down some steps and hit his head and Isabelle remained quiet. Fred would be permanently deaf in that ear, and Isabelle would become somewhat overprotective of her little Fred from then on.

Then Pope John XXIII dies, and then there is Pope Paul VI. This time, Isabelle watches the things about the old and new popes at her mother-in-law's home and they have little tensions. They had come to terms that neither was going to persuade the other. This of course didn't mean she could buy into any of the Catholic thinking, or could they accept her thinking, just that they tolerated one another. Actually, not only did his grandma know she wouldn't change his mom but also she was kind of feeling sorry for her by now and the two of them often acted more like mother and daughter than a Baptist and a Catholic.

The two of them also sit and watched Dr. Martin Luther King Jr. deliver his "I Have a Dream" speech. She even watched a sermon of the Rev. Billy Graham with his mom. They would watch all the world news. After all, Isabelle did not have a TV at home, and they especially found common ground in anything about war. It was now of extra special interest because they had nephews over there, and Isabelle knew Marty may also get drafted. War in general had directly impacted the lives of nearly everyone during these years.

In the midst of the latter part of this time era, the president of the United States, John F. Kennedy was assassinated. This brought a temporary pause to the tensions between everyone. George was still only four years old, although it was unlikely he would remember little about the actual event from his own memory, he would have this event embossed into his memory by the significance it had to those around him. He surely would recall the sorrow of his grandmother and mom, as well as his aunts and uncles, and how they were all together on this.

His mom had once disliked the president for religious reasons, but now seemed to have loved him because of who he was. His dad, on the other hand, was outraged, but not at his mom, but instead to whoever did this, thinking someone in our own government had actually had him killed. They all gathered at his grandma's house for food and drink to watch the funeral on TV. This took the focus off what his mom was doing with him, and George was learning a lot from his mom.

By this time, Isabelle had already taught George his ABCs and his 123s. He learned very fast and was eagerly hungry to learn more. During this time, she was teaching him to count money. He could make change for a dollar from virtually any combination of coins. He could count to one hundred both forward and backward some time before he turned five. She would have to do this without Otto knowing because he was always calling her stupid because she could not read very well and told her the boys were going to take after her. He put her under strict orders not to teach the boys anything because they would grow up to be stupid like her. This made her more determined than ever to show him that the boys were not stupid, especially George.

Otto did not think she could do anything right, including taking care of the bills. They would get behind on things like the gas bill or the rent because she had not paid it on time. Everything bad was her fault, even though he drank up the rent money. He just could not be satisfied with anything she did.

She, on the other hand, knowing she would get the daylight knocked out of her for opening her mouth would just keep trying to save his poor soul. Again, the truth in why this was never a factor before they got married was never fully known. Nevertheless, at this point, she was thoroughly convinced that he was headed straight for hell, and she wanted him to change before it was too late!

This story progressively becomes more difficult to grasp. Before George was five he was getting drunk and what few adults around them didn't think it was funny, at least tolerated it without speaking against Otto. He was not alone; his six-year-old cousin Marie would also get drunk. She would be put up on the bar table with George to dance and the adults all seemed to love it. It was not as if they were committing some secret sin; after all, the priest himself was frequently there and had seen this. This wasn't just at a single bar, but this happened at several local bars, on numerous occasions. The most popular spots were of course the K of C Hall, the VFW Hall, and the American Legion. Both were full of those who had served in the military, as well as many good Catholic folks. In addition, the church actually had what George recalled as a small bar in the basement as part of the kitchen. Such drunkenness was acceptable or at least tolerable in this particular church. Indeed many may find this hard to believe, but it happened.

The children's participation was strictly considered to be no one else's business outside the family. Actually it became quite common for Otto to let them drink from his beer in the bars. At home he had been putting beer in the baby bottles to help them sleep through the night from as early as three months old. He thought beer was good for them, like a vitamin or something and most importantly, in his words, "would keep the brats quiet!" There seemed to be little Isabelle could say about it without taking the bulk of his anger upon herself or possibly the boys, and when she would say something, it never caused him to stop giving them beer, instead it only caused her to be in trouble.

As for Otto's teaching methods, Otto was quick to teach cuss words or dirty songs and jokes. He also taught respect and reverence to him and to our flag, or else. Otto insisted that George should go to the bars and learn about life, because that's what will make a man out of him. In addition, George was now five and a half and Otto insisted on him going to the Catholic school. He did not believe any government-run school could be worth anything. George had already attended the Catholic church preschool where a sister praised Isabelle for her exceptional efforts and accomplishments with him. The nun told her he was a very smart young man. Isabelle got along quite well with the nuns. She respected them a lot and spent hours talking to this one in particular. It was as if religious boundaries were invisible at times, especially with this nun.

Otto had taught George to stand at attention and salute, and to say the Pledge of Allegiance to the Flag, as well as teaching him several dirty songs. George was proving to learn fast. Isabelle, on the other hand, had been teaching him to add and subtract larger numbers before he even went to the Catholic kindergarten. Although she seemed to get along with the nuns very well and even liked a few, deep down she didn't really want George to go to the Catholic school.

She was afraid they would make him a Catholic and her pastor had said they were all going to hell. To help protect him from learning their ways, she felt it was necessary to also involve him in everything the Baptist church had to offer. She had him attend Sunday school and Vacation Bible School. She took the boys to Wednesday evening service at the Baptist church as well as on Sunday evenings. For whatever reason, Otto didn't mind her taking the boys to her church as long as she didn't push its thinking off on him.

The two religions contradicted the other more than Isabelle and Otto. Yes in one church, meant no in the other. This is like taking a driver's test with two instructors and knowing either can fail you. One says turn right, the other says to turn left. You could not possibly pass the driver's test! How could parents be so cruel to a child? A couple factors that would become unforgettable to George was that his mother always went with him to the Baptist church as well as lived out her faith as earnestly as she could before him. That is as she understood it from the Bible and from those who instructed her in the faith.

Meanwhile, his dad cussed at all the churches and he believed all the Baptist preachers were all just hypocrites. But he didn't just pick on her religion; in fact, he especially belittled his own faith, the Catholic church, which he called *the mother tramp*. The priests and bishops were always degraded, and the pope was the top hypocrite of all, and he only had filthy disgusting things to say about the entire group of nuns. Otto refused to go to any church with George, yet insisting upon his attendance to Saturday mass with his grandma. This generated a confused mess. Why should children went to go if the adults would not go to church? This sure confounded this young boy.

His Catholic grandmother, on the other hand, appeared to him as a shining example of true holiness before George. He not only would have no memory of her cussing but also could never remember her even getting mad. She would often tell his mom how she was mistaken, and his mom would return the same. The two of them never really acted mad at one another and never did yell at each other. They would always hug each other when they would see each other. George would go with her to mass on Saturdays and she always gave the warmest hugs. So George also had some very positive Catholic influence in his life as well.

The next thing to come up was Isabelle's trials in wanting to do things with and for the boys. The first zoo in Indianapolis had opened just a few months before, and Isabelle wanted to take the boys there. Otto said no; they couldn't afford such nonsense and only one of the kids was even old enough to remember going, so absolutely no! She would want to go shopping and get the boys toys and different outfits and shoes, and he would say no. Anything she asks he would say no. She would seek guidance from his mom, she would just stay out of it. She was now wondering and asking God, will this ever end? Would He ever help her? Where was He?

Then the Palm Sunday tornadoes came through Indiana and reports came in of several hurt and killed and many would be homeless. Although the storms never directly hit their community it did affect them. The people that had been fussing over little things stopped fussing. Then it was as if there was no black, no white, no Hispanic, no Catholic, no Baptist—just people. Everyone banded together collecting food, clothes, and money. Baptists as well as believers of other faiths would collect things and take them to the Catholic church, then they distributed them. They all simply worked together as one group, united for one cause through this.

George then passes kindergarten with flying colors and it would be on to the first grade next year. The nuns who had worked with George would have nothing but compliments regarding his conduct or character. As for his intelligence, once in a meeting with Mother Superior, she told Isabelle in all her years there, George was thought to have been one of the brightest children she had ever seen. There were absolutely no mentionable issues about George through this point. However, the summer was just beginning. Otto was fired from his current job and stayed at home with the boys while Isabelle worked. This was for most of that summer and changes began to take place.

This process of change was motivating to her first son Marty. Not only did Otto teach him how to become a drinking man but also convinced him that he should go into the military whenever he graduated high school. You see, Otto was constantly slapping his mom around and she just took it and he would hear his mom cry during many nights. Marty on several occasions would try to say or do something and then he would get beaten. Now Marty's rage had built up and he could stand it no more. He told his mom he wanted to kill him.

Then even Isabelle began to believe the military would be a good place for him, and George heard his mom tell Marty that he should join as soon as he can. George was not the only one who heard his mom and brother talking, Otto interrupts and starts to give his input and Marty once again tried to fight Otto; he was much bigger than the last time he tried. He had grown into a big man and thought perhaps he could take him now. He was now somewhat over six feet tall and well over 250 pounds and still seemed to be growing. Unfortunately, his growing size mattered little. Otto kicked the living snot out of this wannabe man. Marty was about seventeen then and would just wait until he got his chance to get away out on his own. George was nearing six when his older brother finally left for the air force.

Rumor was he would have eventually been drafted anyway, but enlisting was the quickest way to get away from home. This was sometime in 1965, and shortly after his basic training, it was off to Vietnam. Somehow he naively thought joining the air force would exclude him from ever being close to any actual battle. He had just lost his best friend in this war and one of his first cousins. The thought of leaving home was a frightening one on its own, but the thought of going to war literally terrified him. Although at eighteen, having now grown into a large man over six feet three and about 275 pounds, he was actually quite timid.

As for the air force not sending him near the war, he was wrong. It placed him at an air base that was way closer to action than he expected. His job was assisting and readying the incoming choppers to leave again. This quickly sickened him. He just couldn't find the stomach for the things he saw. He just wasn't war or hero material. He was deathly afraid. Meanwhile back at home, Otto was very proud of Marty. He kept saying the military was going to make a man out of him. He claimed that it was his parenting that motivated him to do what every man should do and go serve this great country.

Otto was always big on telling stories that revolved around the war, but would generally keep the details of war itself silent. Oh sure he would tell, "We kicked their butts," "Yeah, we won, we won!" But the actual acts of war that had lined his mind with scars he spoke little of unless he was drinking the strong stuff. When he drank beer, he was a happy drunk. He would laugh, joke, and tell of the many ladies he was with and all the places he went. Especially now with Marty in the military, he filled the bar conversation with his typical war stories and how proud he was that Marty would get some stories of his own. Marty, on the other hand, just wished he would die or wished that his mom would just leave him before Otto killed her.

By this time, there was so much stress in the home that their marriage was but a word. Otto's baby sister Anna was kind enough to watch the boys so that Isabelle and Otto could go out on the town alone to try to rebuild their obviously broken relationship. Anna was secretly a lesbian. She had been repeatedly raped by Otto when she was a small child. Otto attempted to prove that his sexual identity was the opposite of his aggressor by aggressively having the opposite sex.

Anna reacted differently, especially after learning of the death of her son, which she never really even got to know. She did not want an adult man. Anna would have a girlfriend over and would have the boys, George and Fred, to watch them. This started when George was very young.

This could perhaps have partially been out of revenge toward Otto for what he had done to her. Anna and her friend would do sexual things to each other and have George try to reenact them with his little four-and-a-half-year-old brother. They told him to keep this a secret, and he would always have a fun time with them. It was interesting and seemed fun, so he did. He and his little brother would go home and conduct more secret experiments of their own.

Meanwhile, the visits to the bar never ceased. On several occasions, George had witnessed the priest being very drunk. You see, the priest and Otto were excellent drinking buddies. George knew this because up until now, three to four evenings a week and most weekends much to Isabelle's disapproval, Otto took him to the bar.

George witnessed the priest falling asleep at the bar several times. He recalls seeing him get sick all over the place and even falling down a flight of stairs at the church once because he was too drunk to walk. George had heard the priest use some of the same foul language as Otto; words his mom would say would send you to hell for saying. George not only witnessed this but also on several occasions heard the Baptist preacher say drunkards cannot go to heaven. At this point believing his mom was right, he had all sorts of thoughts going on.

This combined with another of his dad's views of the Catholic church: it is worthless beyond being a babysitter for kids. It was inevitable that George would rebel against the Catholic church. The first three quarters of his first grade year his grades were straight As, but then his attention flew south, and when it finally migrated back, it was with a vengeance. As for Otto, helping with the kids in any way from this point on would never be in a positive way.

4

Going It Alone!

At just after his seventh birthday, George found himself in trouble with his teacher, which was, of course, a nun. When she instructed the class to print, he would write in cursive. She would be teaching the class to add and subtract, while he was learning to divide, or copying out his multiplication tables. While the class would read, he would draw pictures on his desk. When the class would color, he would carve small sculptures from the crayons.

He found this schooling to be very annoying. With Isabelle having already taught him to not only quote the Lord's Prayer and the twenty-third Psalm but also he knew the alphabet; he could add, subtract, and he knew his multiplication tables through twelve. She had also been teaching him to divide. Most she had taught him before he even went to the first grade. However, she could not teach him to read much because she could barely read herself. He quickly grasped how to read the first-grade level books and then became very bored with his time in the classroom.

During this time era, little consideration was given regarding the possibilities of gifted children coming from within the lower income areas. In addition, little was said about the effects of a child being hyperactive or having ADHD that is unless you were from the other side of the tracks, so to speak!

Children produced from the lower-income level and from virtually uneducated parents were seldom thought to be capable of achieving much. But they were certainly not going to be considered as being as smart as children from the well-to-do homes which had educated parents. Also, hyperactive children from this side of the tracks were thought to just be another mental case or a product of their environment. Therefore, in total blindness to the whole picture, the only prognosis was to assume that George was in fact very disturbed and without the proper discipline would end up like his father or worse.

This nun had tried to be patient with George. He would always recall her as having been kind consistently, but he did not want her kindness. Until now, she had not been mean or cruel to George, and now she was just becoming a victim herself. George had stolen some Limburger cheese, and at the end of a cold winter day, he smeared it down into several of the heat registers. This nose-curling smell prevented class for everyone that next day. When the sister asked who did it, George stood up and proudly said, "I did," and with a bold attitude asked, "What are you going to do about it, witch?"

This nun's patience had finally been broken. The sanctioned form of discipline was a leather strap across the palm of the hands. This strapping had already become a regular event from other sisters, but till now this one had kept trying to be Ms. Nice. Although, this time, George would remember that this sister had tears in her eyes.

George's rebellious attitude was just charging up. He had begun forming a habit of exploding into raging fits and was becoming impossible to intimidate into submission. Displaying the guts for anything, he begins cussing her and other nuns out! Occasionally she would find the need to physically drag him to Mother Superior's office. Everyone, including the much-older kids, were afraid of her, that is everyone but George.

Most would have only been her office once but not George. These confrontations progressed to the point that his hands would swell up so much from the lashes that they looked deformed at times. Once he recalled that he could not even shut his hands to hold a pencil, and received more lashes for not writing. Stubbornly he would just further provoke them to hit him again and again.

This came to an end one day with an unbelievable boldness in an eye-to-eye confrontation. George did more than just cuss out Mother Superior, he accused her of sleeping with the priest because his dad said she probably did! George described the alleged act clearly and in gross detail. George was severely lashed for this. With his hands blisteringly red, he was then sent to face the priest. Instead of conforming to the expected repentant attitude, George boldly told the priest that he was a drunken hypocrite, cussed him out, and told him that he was headed straight for hell! (He heard the Baptist minister and his mother said where the priest was headed).

They said that George must be possessed by the devil. They just could not do anything with him. Isabelle thought that the fact that they did not even try to perform an exorcism on him to cast out any demon they said he was possessed by only proved they were not the holy people they claimed to be. She thought this because she had heard about the power to cast out demons from a Holy Roller. One of Isabelle's brothers, Steven (a radical Oneness Pentecostal), would occasionally visit and tell them about how the Catholic and Baptist churches were both wrong and, of course, how he was so right, how the other religions possessed no power, and how he had power from God Almighty! Of course he never cast any demons out of George or Otto either. Steven actually died about a year after this incident from Huntington's disease.

Perhaps in total ignorance, the Catholic priest neglected to consider that George's "words" were in fact true to George. They were not just a fabrication in his mind but were more so that George was relaying a combination of the opinions of others; George was such a religiously mixed-up child. He was given a venomous combination of insight regarding who God was and just who were God's people.

He also had other family members who were Methodists, Lutherans, Pentecostals, as well as those from other belief systems such as the Mormons and the Jehovah's Witnesses. They all naturally felt it their duty to share their input with poor Isabelle about what was wrong with her little George, and because nothing seemed to work, when possible she would occasionally try things their way. That is until she would see that their way didn't work either.

Regardless of what circumstances had contributed to him being this way, the Catholic church and the school would no longer tolerate it. They chose to protect all the other good little apples from this very wormy one. They said George was the worst example of a child that this Catholic school had ever known. This particular school was deep within the poverty-stricken inner city; it was a high-crime rate area that had a history of producing bad apples, and they said George was the worst they had ever had.

At just seven years old, George was permanently expelled from the Catholic school system. Isabelle was told to just keep him at home; he was not welcome or even permitted to be on any of this school or church properties ever again. "Just keep him at home! Forget about first communion, it could never be for him. He was just plain evil!" This was relayed straight from the priest's mouth. Was this how the Catholic church operates or believes? Absolutely not! No more than the Baptist belief would promote or condone everything Isabelle's pastor did, or neglected to do. But this stuff really did happen.

Being as the law required that children attend school, this, of course, caused the proper juvenile authorities to get involved. One day a juvenile officer came to their home asking questions. Fortunately for the juvenile officer, Otto was at work. He spoke with Isabelle, inquiring her side of the story, and without the intimidation of Otto there, she opened up and told him the story.

The officer said that, at some point soon, Otto and her would be required to go to court. George overhearing this then told the officer he was going to tell his dad and he would whip his XYZ! This while Isabelle tried to silence George and not necessarily make an excuse for, but explain George's foul mouth. She was afraid the officer would just take the boys from her right then for his acting up like that, but he said he understood. He assured Isabelle it would get better after the court hearing, and that the police would be there in a hurry if she needed them.

Within what seemed to just be a few days, this all resulted in a court hearing requiring George and both parents to be present. Otto, of course, was drunk for just such an occasion and before the hearing was even to start they arrested Otto for his loud and rude behavior. It took four officers to detain him. This had all taken place in the courtroom before the judge had even come out.

After the judge reviewed the case, he spoke with Isabelle for a while. Then he asked George to sit next to him, and he kindly asked George where he had learned such vulgarity. George told the judge that it was from his dad, George then cussed out the judge and said that his dad was going to whip the judge's "xyz!" for putting his "blinking" nose where it did not "blinking" belong, and if he ever puts his nose where it did not belong again, his dad was going to cut off his "abcde" and feed them to him! The judge quickly ruled that Otto was an unfit father. He then gave Isabelle an ultimatum to immediately remove Otto from the home, or the court would remove the children.

Furthermore, George was to undergo a court-ordered psychological examination. He was to begin any necessary psychological treatment before permitting him to enter the public school system. A court-appointed caseworker was to be assigned to monitor the case; obtaining reports from the psychologist, verifying the appointments were kept, and to report back to the judge if there were any issues. Isabelle was instructed go to the caseworker's office, once a month alone and once a month with George. The caseworker was also to make a monthly visit to their home.

She felt this whole thing was like placing her in a very tiny boat, in a raging white water river with sharp rocks extending from the very deep and swift water, while binding one arm and throwing those she loved who could not even swim overboard on each side of her in such dangerous waters. She had to choose quickly or all those she loved would drown. Of course, she chose the boys over her abusive husband and then to face the many changes and challenges that were to come with that decision.

One such change was that until now Isabelle had worked but had just lost her job. She was fired due to her recent decline in attendance. By now her pride was all but nonexistent and she and the boys would be forced to apply for and rely on the welfare and food stamp program. In addition, her every idle moment was tuned in to the latest news in Vietnam, because her oldest son Marty was out there somewhere. George would frequently overhear Isabelle talking to people, explaining that it was all because George would not behave. George was to blame for her missing so much work.

There were the many visits to the schools, the courts, the psychologists, and visits to the state aid office and visits from the state social worker. This period caused Isabelle to undergo many changes. This included a rapid decline in her own emotional and physical health. She was on several nerve pills for the stress and depression, as well as experiencing some physical problems. Within months, she would undergo a complete hysterectomy.

With her own physical and emotional strength nearing total exhaustion, she needed support from others now more than ever. However, she was now an outcast from the family. The only family she had living close was from Otto's side who thought she was wrong to leave her husband: "Put him above all others," this was in her vow and she had turned from it so she was shunned, so to speak.

This, of course, was not an excommunication sanctioned by the church because she was never a Catholic. However it produced the actions much like the Amish shunning. Catholic families and friends within this particular environment often reacted in like ways. It would seem that you're family only as long as you fit their mold. She could expect to find her own way from here on, just as when her parents had died.

Yes, the boy's grandmother still loved them and Otto's sister, the boys' godmother (Anna the lesbian), was still happy to watch the kids anytime. However, it was not without being very judgmental and critical of Isabelle's every action. God's wrath was going to be unleashed upon Isabelle for betraying her vows. They were always belittling her to George. In front of the boys, they also repeatedly told Isabelle that her disobedience was placing a curse on her and the boys and they could not and would not give her or the boys any spiritual support if she divorced her husband for anything less than adultery.

She didn't believe there were any other exceptions that excused or gave her permission for granting a divorce. This was not only the Catholic belief but also that of the Baptist faith as well. Neither religion would approve of a divorce for abuse or because one just didn't want to be married to the other, and then permit her to a single person's freedom. Otto was many things but had always been sexually faithful to Isabelle, so the only spiritual support she could get was toward a legal separation. Otto, on the other hand, as a Catholic could seek an annulment because she was not Catholic; however, he never did want a divorce.

This certainly seemed to bury Otto further into the bottle and likewise it was like placing Isabelle on death row, in an inescapable prison. Neither of their convictions would permit freedom from the other. As for Otto, the bottle would hold the answer to his anguish. As for Isabelle, her physical and emotional need for a male companion and helpmate was to be unfulfilled forever or she must go against God and her church.

It quickly became an inner belief of Isabelle that this was a type of godsent judgment or a kind of sentence for failing to get Otto saved. She was to raise the boys alone in a very high-crime and poverty-stricken community. She was to accomplish this task-facing obstacles such as having virtually no formal education herself, combined with an over forty-year age gap to the children. This was magnified by being socially and culturally out of touch with modern city living, for she was still considered by many as a backwoods hillbilly.

Adapting to single parenting would prove to be a long and very tiring process. However, it was quickly understood that life for her and the boys had changed. Up until now, everything was in Otto's name. Now she had to secure a place to live and get utilities on in her name. She literally had no clue as to what to do. There appeared to be no help with this task; no help from family or from the Catholic church, and only limited help from her church. She went on a bus to the County Welfare Office where they said they could get her on food stamps and over the course of a couple weeks they could get her started on state aid, but nothing that day!

The initial help came from a total stranger; a lady she had met on a bus home from a visit to the welfare office. Isabelle was crying and a woman offered her a handkerchief, asking her what was wrong. Isabelle unloaded her burden and the woman cried and prayed with her. The lady wrote Isabelle a check for three hundred dollars, which at that time was a lot of money especially for a stranger to just give someone. She told Isabelle if she ever was in the position to help someone else, then she could do the same for someone someday. Isabelle graciously promised to do just that.

As the days became weeks, she and the boys had settled into an apartment within the same school district to cut down on the changes. It was about three blocks from a store and had a small backyard that the landlord told her she could use to raise a vegetable garden in. One of the ladies from her church had gotten a new washing machine and gave Isabelle her ringer-type washer.

She had always had to do the grocery shopping and housework any way, but now the boy's grandma and aunt would watch the boys at their convenience, not hers. It was obvious that when it was time for her to go shopping they would not watch the boys to cause her grief to make her realize she had it better with Otto. She walked to the store and pulled a cart back and forth with a five- and a seven-year-old. She had to deal with the boys wanting things in the store she could not buy. Little Fred was well behaved, but George would, on several occasions, throw tantrums in the store when she would not get him whatever he wanted, resulting in his pants getting dropped right there in the store.

She was so thankful she could at least do the laundry at home with her own washing machine, using wash tubs to rinse the clothes, and clotheslines to dry them. She would make homemade laundry soap. And the baking and cooking never seemed to stop. There was no store-bought bread or canned biscuits. Any form of bread was always homemade, and virtually every vegetable they were to eat, she would grow and can herself.

From the outside looking in you would assume cooking and gardening were her hobbies, but it was a lot of hard and very necessary work. Then there was the measles, the mumps, chickenpox, and runny noses to tonsillitis with the boys. Getting them up and ready for school, to dealing with doctors and teachers while all the above was still to be done. Then there was trying to have presents for the boys on their birthdays, for Christmas, or trying to dress them nice for Easter Sunday at church or for school pictures. But over that past year, through it all she also faithfully attended every church service with the boys.

As for the boys, little Fred was now in preschool and doing fine. This was her baby, and although she hated him going to school, this gave her some much-needed time for herself. Then there was Marty, she would write several letters, many she could not send because she couldn't afford stamps. The letters from Vietnam were few. She would often try listening to the radio for the latest news about the war. As for George, he had completed the court-ordered psychological testing, and he and his mom were weekly going to see a psychologist. George was now enrolled in the first grade in the public school.

They had nearly sent him into the second grade because his grades from the Catholic school had been straight A's, except for conduct. George was quite capable of doing second-grade work. But in light of his behavior and the fact that he had also missed nearly sixty days of the prior school year they chose to hold him back.

This change was also his first experience in the public school and it started with him, a seven-and-a-half-year-old in the first grade, thinking that "God," the church community, the school system, the legal system, and all those who represent the law, as well as his parents, were now his enemies. You could say that he had a criminal or rebellious mind-set or the ingredients to form one. But from this point on, there would be no speculations as to how he was; that answer was soon very clear—he was just plain mean. And now a year older than many in his class. The process of peer domination begins.

As part of the court order, George was to continue undergoing any mental treatment needed after the evaluation that was suggested as a result of the evaluation. The psychologist felt it necessary to experiment with trying different drugs on George. Well before he was to turn eight, he was on prescribed "dope," while simultaneously going to the bars and sipping on dad's beer.

Surely no competent thinking person really believed dear old dad would no longer influence little George! This explosive combination just magnified his emotional instabilities. The combination of such drugs as Ritalin and alcohol would mess up anyone's mind.

This eventually made George's memory unreliable; filled with many fragmented, faded, or even totally blocked-out incidents of this time period. This shifted the reasons for getting into trouble in school from mouthing off to simply falling asleep in class. He would frequently lack the ability to be attentive. Even he would have been willing to learn, but at times he simply could not mentally function as a normal child should.

The actual court order was that Otto be removed from the home, and that a legal process to exclude him from the home be immediately underway. In a nutshell, Isabelle was to just file for a legal separation then and there, and not have him back in the home. It was ordered at that time, that until stated by another judge that Otto not have any visitations with the boys.

Within just a few days, it was a different judge who put the legal separation in effect, and as part of this, he gave visitation rights to Otto. The only stipulations were that it was not to be at Isabelle's place of residence and that she had to agree where the visits would be.

This proved to be catastrophic to say the least. Much of the time this would be in environments that placed him in the care of intoxicated people or those whose influence and actions were sexually abusive. Granted, the judge knew nothing of the sexual abuse, but the alcohol was a definite factor. Given the record, the judge should have at the very least dictated that visitation was not to be permitted while under the influence of alcohol, but he did not!

Sometime just before he was eight years old, he felt the sexual playtime with his aunt and her friend was not fun anymore. In fact George was learning the definitions of things, and he knew he did not want to be gay! Up till now this was the only mentionable or memorable fun time for George, and now what would it become? The sexual experiments with his little brother stops about this time. Although the incidents with his aunt do not stop yet, they somewhat begin to lessen. From this point on, his enragement started producing more extremely bitter feelings and violent actions. And his grades worsened reflecting the problems were progressing.

Finally it was now summer break and George was going to be pushed into the second grade next year by the rules of the time, not by merit. His grades were Ds and Fs, but the system limited a child to but two years in each grade. They suggested summer school, but Isabelle was sent some train tickets from her Mormon sister in Utah for her and George to come and see her; she could not leave him with no one.

She had written Marty letters and was keeping him informed as to how things were going, but seldom would she receive letters from Marty. He wrote one letter that only said, "I want to come home." She missed him so and felt so afraid for him. Her ears were tuned in at all times for the latest news about the war. She wished so much that he was home. He could really be of help to her now; no one would watch both the boys and she really could use a break.

She left little Fred with his grandma because George was all she could handle, and Fred was such a sweet baby he would not be any trouble for his grandma. So they then set out for Utah. The trip was full of excitement and fun for George, but not for Isabelle. Her sister and her husband were Mormons and began trying to brainwash her into believing that everything that happened was her fault and that it would never be better unless she became a Mormon.

She was so stressed out from this exposure that she called yet another of her sisters in California, who was also a Southern Baptist. She then drove to Utah and there was a big argument, and she took Isabelle and George back to California with her. Then Isabelle was given the rundown from her on what she should and shouldn't do. While they were there, his aunt and uncle took them to Yosemite National Park. On this trip, they seen the big redwood trees, some waterfalls, and they went to the ocean before it was all over. Then they paid for a bus ticket for them to get back home.

This was a very memorable trip for George, they were gone for nearly six weeks. Now back home, Isabelle found that Otto had been visiting little Fred nearly every day. She had left him with the clear understanding that he was not to be around Fred. She was in a heated state to say the least. Then Otto shows up with new bikes for the boys, a sack of new clothes for when the boys started school, and he had some money for Isabelle; he was sober and told her he had changed. The next thing you know, after being apart for over a year, they were back together.

Bam! Right away, one of the things Otto had a problem with was that he worked a night shift and the boys would not let him sleep. This was an excuse for a nightcap to help him sleep. She nearly had him removed but his statement to Isabelle was, that with school soon to be back in session and little Fred now going to start kindergarten it won't be a problem. He wouldn't have to drink whiskey to get to sleep then. That's when he got the meanest, when he drank the strong stuff. Beer never seemed to make him angry, it was the whiskey. Why in the world she bought that line is beyond any logical explanation.

Around this time, George began to wet the bed. After having not had that problem since he was about two or three, it was thought that George was doing this out of spite. This meant that it was to be a discipline issue and George needed to be taught a lesson. Otto wanted to slam the window on it, if you know what I mean. Isabelle insisted she would handle it! The lessons she gave aggressed when he did not stop: on the weekends, he would be made to lie in the wet bed until the sheets actually had thoroughly dried. But after school would start that would not do for a school day, that is unless he was home under an expulsion from school.

A psychologist, of all people, recommended to Isabelle that she threaten to place his wet sheet outside where his peers would see it. The intent was that through a fear of embarrassment that he would make a conscious decision to quit wetting the bed. Well, it did not work. George was just too drugged to wake up to go to the restroom.

Beautiful! The doctors gave him a handful of pills to take before bed and instructed they be taken with plenty of water. Some of which had side effects of giving him a dry mouth, making him want to drink even more, while putting him into a very deep sleep.

Although realistically, the psychologist likely would have sanctioned only a bluff, they should have read Isabelle well enough to understand that if she said she would do something, she would feel obligated to make good on her word. Nearly every day he would wet the bed and his wet sheet hung in the front yard. His little brother would make sure that the other children saw and knew it was George's.

Meanwhile, Marty is given a medical discharged from the air force; no wounds, no explanation. All that was known is he was out, and now he was on nerve pills! This outraged Otto. His pride was now turned to disgrace toward Marty. He felt he should be put in front of a firing squad and shot like a deserting coward. Otto felt a man is not a real American unless he is willing to serve this land with guts. He felt Marty was just a crying coward who had just missed his mommy so much he had a nervous breakdown!

From this point on, Otto refused to acknowledge that Marty even existed. He absolutely refused to even let Marty come to the house. Isabelle had been consumed with spending every idle moment listening to news about the war because she had feared losing Marty. Now with him safe she was relieved, but Otto running him off was like putting all but the final nail into their marriage. The final nail was driven shortly after this.

It had actually only been about three months after Otto had come back home. One day, Otto gave George the beating of his life because he wet the bed; he threatened to slam the window on *it*, stating that is what it may take to get him to stop wetting the bed. Although Otto had let him drink a whole beer right before he went to bed the night before, Otto said he was just too lazy to get out of bed. Isabelle had finally had it with him. While he was at work that night, she threw his clothes out into the yard and had the police be there when Otto got home from work the next morning.

The police instructed him to leave and to stay away, and he hit one of the officers. This ended in George seeing the police take his dad away again, and he felt it was because he wet the bed. Many similar incidents George found to be confusing; he just could not understand why it was okay for his mom to beat him, but it was not okay for his dad to. He loved his dad too and it just never made sense to him why the police had to take him.

Up until now, they had only been legally separated. Otto was not even supposed to be around the boys at their home. Somehow he had once again weaseled his way back in, but this time Isabelle was headstrong about ending this drama. This time Isabelle was really done; she immediately started trying to fix this by filing for a divorce.

Otto spent the next thirty days in jail and was told if he would not go along with the divorce he may never see his boys again. He was also told that Isabelle may also lose the boys should he not go along with the divorce. He was told that he would at least get visitation rights through a divorce and she could keep the kids. He then accepts that this may be the best choice and makes what he called the toughest decision he ever made. The divorce would not come for nearly a year, and until it was to be final, his visitation with the boys was very limited. This extra time also gave him and his family some hope that a divorce would not actually come.

5

Why?

George now felt rejected by his dad through his abandonment. George knew his dad could see them every other week but he just didn't. He had not seen his dad for over three months, and this further sent George over the edge. Now it was permanent. His dad was gone from home forever and his mom and the stupid law did it. It was over all the stupid religious junk that they all fussed about. It was his mom's preacher's fault, because he said the priest was going to hell. It was the priest's fault for being a drunkard. It was this teacher's fault or that nun's fault. Who knows, but one thing was for sure in George's mind, it was someone's fault.

His mom would be flakey and unclear about whose fault, or why it happened. One minute it was his dad's fault, then it was all George's fault. He then begins thinking his mom did this for his older brother Marty, but Marty had left and no longer would stay with them. Marty was having issues of his own; feeling angry toward his mom because he felt she had put him last. As for George, his mom and dad were now divorced and all he could understand was it was somehow someone's fault. But whose? And why did it all happen, why?

At this point in time, George began figuring out who to blame. It was a combination that always included himself. It was his brother's fault, the judge's, the police's, the different churches' or the priest's, the nun's, his mom's preacher or Sunday school teacher, the public school teachers' or the doctors', and of course his mom's fault!

All the educated folks of the time stood idly by scratching their heads as to why George was becoming so mean! Now at eight and a half years old, he started the second grade, and they quickly would repeat the same question they had been asking for over three years, "Why was he so ornery?" Now it had just gotten much worse with no apparent answer to that famous question, "Why?" Why would he drive pencils into the stomachs of other children, look them in the eye, and say, "Die!"?

As if amazed with wonder, the so-called smart folks just wondered why! Why would he bite part of one's ear off? Why would he catch one's shirt on fire? Why would he try putting mouse poison in another's food? What would possess him to be so wicked or cruel? Well, kids can be cruel; George was one and without a recognizable excuse, so they said. Isabelle was assured he merely just needed firm and consistent discipline! She would primarily be influenced by some teachers who found pleasure in beating George with a wooden paddle until he could not sit! His behavior was then to blame for yet flunking another year at school, the second grade.

There seemed to be a different punishment for each thing George did wrong. Isabelle, being from the backwoods, not only knew old ways but also they were her preference. She made homemade lye soap. This was used for washing clothes and bathing. Isabelle had found another use for her lye soap. Now at over nine years old, she would wash George's mouth out with it for cussing. Often bloodying his mouth and making him very sick. If George cussed her out, as he often did, she would have him take three or four tablespoons of castor oil. If he spit it out or did not take it willingly, she would get him down on the floor, sit on him, holding his nose until he gasped for air, and then would pour the whole bottle down him.

The physical restraining and forceful submission became the norm and near-daily routine until he became strong enough to withstand her, or would just outmaneuver her to temporarily escape. He grew to be an infuriated young lad and his nature became more like a rattlesnake than that of a human. His pain tolerance was ever-growing and would now surpass many adults. He would do senseless things to show off his pain tolerance. He would put cigarettes out on his arm without blinking. He took a cake out of the oven without pot holders causing blisters on his hands, and he didn't flinch. Another time he took his own stitches out once, and tried to stitch himself up another time. But each of these times he was way out there on the psycho meds. Once when he had no meds, street drugs, or booze, he stubbed his toe and his mom said he whined like a baby.

The circumstances appeared to control everything except his attitude. It was somehow completely overlooked that it was many of these very circumstances that were responsible for the core of his rebellion. He felt his rebellion was a sure way he could show others who tried to control him, that they had no control. They could control everything else but they would not get him to willingly conform; he would not be broken. With each opportunity, he would try to get away to just have what he would call some fun! Naturally, such a list of fun things would be constructed from whatever he was told he was forbidden to do.

The churches were unified in the news. The governor of California, Ronald Reagan, signed a bill legalizing the California abortion law. And the largest voice against this was the Catholic church, and the Baptists were in the background saying "amen" to the voice of the Catholics. The two religions were united in this belief, along with every other Christian church; it was clearly wrong to kill babies. Nearly no Christian religions even believed in any form of birth control at this time, let alone abortion.

Not long after this time, his dad comes by with one of his aunts and uncles. They explained that Robert Kennedy was going to speak and wanted Isabelle to go. George would have to go also, and Fred could stay with grandma. None of them actually knew it at this time but earlier Dr. Martin Luther King was assassinated.

People were eager to hear from Mr. Kennedy, because of the recent rise in rascal issues and tension. But when he spoke to the crowd that was almost all black, he told of the assassination. Although absolutely everyone there was sorrowful at the loss of Dr. King, the crowd expressed cheers in unity at his ending words. Otto said he was going to finally vote, and that man would get his vote. But within just a couple months, he too was assassinated.

Shortly after this, the divorce was finalized. As part of the divorce, Otto was given legal visitation rights; however, this time he was not to be under the influence of alcohol during any such visitation. Otto quickly felt he was lied to; this was absolutely not part of a deal he made. The judge added this as part of the custody agreement after he agreed to the divorce. This quickly sent Otto into a state of outrage and resulted in another thirty days in jail. After his release the next six or eight months, he was on a drinking spell. He never even tried to see the boys during this time.

During these months the racial tension in the area was growing. George was slowly losing some of his black friends, but not by his choice. Their parents didn't want them hanging out with George because he was white. George was always in fights, but he hadn't fought with others about color until this time period. Also, George was mostly the one starting fights and picking on others, but now he was being picked on because he was white. The whole racial thing never did make sense to George but he wasn't going to be picked on either, so a fight was on.

As time passes now into the next spring, his older brother began to come by once in a while. He had taken George to drive-ins and to the theater to see movies. They went to a couple of drag races, and to an Indy race. But about this time he was talking about the big event coming up later that summer at Woodstock. He was going and George wanted to go too, but he was not old enough. His brother promised to bring him something from The Who if he managed to get to see them. This was the group the two of them listened to when they smoked dope together.

With summer vacation now here again, Isabelle had caught George's fascination with the many stories of life in the backwoods of Missouri. She had a brother John, who had lost his wife and son through a divorce several years back. For several years after the war, she actually had no idea what had even happened to him. She had heard he married and had a son, but until a couple years before, hadn't seen him since the war. Over the last couple of years, they would get to see him on occasion. He had moved back to Missouri, in fact just a few miles from the old homeplace.

With both her physical and mental health in need of some time away from George, her brother said he would be glad to take him for the summer. Her brother, John, was practically deaf and did not drive, so he came to see her on a bus and then took George back with him. His hearing was severely damaged by a loud explosion during WWII in Europe. He wore hearing aids in both ears and you would have to yell for him to even hear you a little.

Meanwhile, while George was away, Isabelle received a letter from her baby sister that she would come visit them later that year. She wanted to catch up on all they had missed since the last time they saw each other some twenty years earlier. This was just the refreshing thing Isabelle needed. Actually, she was ready for a mental hospital from everything and just the idea of getting to see her sister made her summer a refreshing one.

As for George, he liked his uncle. He was always laughing and often acted more like a kid than an adult. They played a lot of checkers and dominoes and such. Staying on the farm was also a lot of fun because here there were but two rules: One was, don't leave the farm, and the second was don't tear up stuff. That was going to be easy, because as for leaving he would have to walk a long way, and there really was not a whole lot to tear up; just a whole lot of fun stuff to do.

Isabelle had brought George and his little brother to the farm several different times for a weekend at a time. Marty hadn't gone on any of these trips. He was long gone into drugs and rock and roll. This was the most relaxing getaways ever and always fun and something new always happened. Alcohol and illegal drugs were not needed. Actually for the most part, even the prescription drugs were not used. There was plenty to keep their minds off the life at home.

They would all go pick berries and nuts. They also picked plums, peaches, pears, and apples. This was always fun. The thing that was the sweetest and George's favorite were the strawberries. The thing that was the most sour, were the gooseberries. The thing that was the most bitter, were the persimmons. Once when they were blackberry picking, his uncle John got sprayed by a skunk. Boy did that stink! That made for a whole lot of laughs for a long time.

Another time when they got back to his camper trailer, George's mom opened a kitchen cabinet and there was about a four-foot-long black snake inside. She then reached in and grabbed it and took it to the back door and threw it out. They would not kill a black snake even if it kept getting the eggs out of the chicken house, or in this case even into the house you stayed in. This was because they said the nonpoisonous snakes helped keep the poisonous ones away. But it sure was fun to get to see their mom scared. She said she wasn't, but even though she grabbed the snake, she did scream and the boys thought that was funny and so did their uncle John. Their uncle made a bit of a game out of trying to scare her the rest of that day.

This area was really infested with copperhead snakes, and their uncle would kill one or more timber rattlesnakes each year. They would always warn the boys to watch close near the water because he had also killed three cottonmouths just that year.

George did not know what this summer would hold but he knew it would be fun. This time was going to be different because he was there with just his uncle John. His mom made sure his uncle took enough of his medicines to last him all summer. His uncle just trusted George to take it on his own. He would occasionally ask if he had taken it, and that was that, and the fun begins.

He was building a new house on eighty acres surrounded by forest. He lived in a big camper. It had electricity, and he had a cesspool dug for the drain from the sink and bathroom. But they would have to go down to the spring about a hundred yards and get buckets of water because his uncle did not have a well yet. All the indoor plumbing was done, but the water was just not there yet. This was not that much work because his uncle went too, and they would take the fishing poles; wade the shallows in search of crawdads for bait and then fish for a while. He would let him go swimming in the creek before they brought the water up the hill.

George's mom had already taught him to shoot a .22-caliber rifle but this summer was going to be a lot different because his uncle had quite the gun collection. He told him that if he behaved that one at a time he would get to shoot several of them before the summer was over. George had one gun in particular in mind, it was a .30-06 he had seen his mom shoot an apple with one time.

First he gave him a single shot .410, taught him how to hold, carry, clean, and load the shotgun. Then after what seemed to be a daylong lesson in safety, his uncle places two sandstones about the size of a baseball a ways apart from each other, in the branches of a tree. Then he has George take aim. He struggles to even lift it into position but he does and shoots. George thought, *Wow, what a powerful gun.* It broke the stone into three pieces, and it had a massive kick and everything.

Then his uncle lifted his shotgun with George standing close beside him, focused on the other rock, and *kaboom!* It was absolutely the loudest thing George had ever heard and the other stone had completely disappeared. It had just instantly turned into a dust cloud and was gone! His uncle John had used an 8-gauge shotgun. He then told George that if he did as he said, he would have him shooting that gun by the time he reached twelve.

He had George willing to be a follower, and he kept his word. Every three or four days he was learning about and trying a new gun. After a couple weeks, he gave George five boxes of one hundred .22-caliber shells and the bolt action .22 his mother had taught him to use. He said, "Go practice, because tomorrow you are going hunting." He had set George up a shooting range and he spent most all day with that five hundred shots and his arm was so tired and in pain from holding the rifle that he did not want to shoot anymore and really did not wish to go hunting.

Well, that was okay with his uncle. It was just another poke of fun he had at the city boy. After listening to him call him a baby, the next day they went squirrel hunting. His uncle got five and George got two. They went back to the camper and he had George help skin them. *Yuck*, he thought. Then it was on to the job of stirring the squirrel and dumplings, and George drew the line when it came to eating them. He just kept seeing a rat swimming around in the pot. He thought that they looked like the alley rats from the dumpsters in the city. He just could not eat that.

Over the course of this summer, his uncle had not just let him shoot several guns but taught him how to handle, care for, and respect their power. These guns were a single-shot .22, a bolt-action .22 with a clip, a single-shot .410, a .22 automatic, and a .25 two-shot derringer pistol, and he got to hold the ones he would get to shoot the next time he would visit. George was also allowed to hold the .30-06 he wanted to shoot, but his uncle said he had to show him he could be patient first. That one would have to be another time.

The farm was seventeen miles from town. They would have to walk about four miles once a week to his uncle's friend's house and they would give them a ride to the store and back home. George didn't think this was all bad because they had a granddaughter who was nearly two years older than George, and the two of them hit it off quickly. She was somewhat going through a boy-crazy stage much earlier than she should.

Although she was a good deal older than George she was fascinated by him. During his visits around her, she had told George of the things her own dad had been doing to her and likewise he told her about his aunt. The two of them became friends in more than one way that summer. The older folks were just plain blind to what went on and this was never known. While they talked about the cows or pigs, or how the gardens were, the kids would go play house in a field.

Other than this weekly bit of evil stupidity, things had gone quite well during his visit. This summer had been a lot of fun and the funny thing was that he had no booze, no illegal drugs, and actually even had seldom taken his prescribed medication. This would confound the modern head doctors of the time, because he did not cause his uncle any mentionable problems. Oh, he did things wrong that his uncle just did not know about, and as for the medication he was supposed to be taking, he had saved it because he knew he could sell or trade it for things like bikes and stuff when he got back home.

Now back home, it was as if the peace he found in the outdoors was forgotten, everything was back to normal. This included the stress on his mom. She got him enrolled in school, now nine and a half years old he was going into the second grade for the second time. This was going to produce some interesting issues for sure. Mentally, George was anything but normal for his age. Although academically, he was far behind, he was far advanced in many ways. His ability to outthink even adults proved to be a constant stress for Isabelle. Then Isabelle received a letter from her sister telling her she would be there the next week. This put the pressure from his ignorance on hold. She just kept thinking about her sister coming.

Finally his aunt Rebecca arrives, who also had a problem child named Jimmy. He had just turned ten years old and he and George seemed to hit it off just fine. George had to go to school and his cousin was not going to start school for another week, so the second day of school George played hooky. They played ball, they rode bikes, and they played with some Hot Wheels in the dirt, and then they ventured off exploring over by the train yard.

George and his ten-year-old cousin Jimmy then hopped a train and went to the end of the line, which was just a few miles to a turntable. They were caught by the engineer. He talked friendly to them and got them to tell him their real names and where they lived. He didn't talk to them like they were in trouble or anything, he just seemed to want to get to know them. They were too excited to realize that while he was pretending to be nice, someone else was calling George's mom. The railroad workers at the turntable explained how it all worked.

They said to take a good look because the railroad was having trouble and may shut down to never work again. They had quite a field trip full of memorable history that day. The engineer showed them how the big diesel motor turned the generator, how the generator supplied electric to the drive motors that actually made the engine go down the tracks. He then put them up in the engine and away they went. He let them think they were driving the train back to where they had gotten on. When they got off the train, there was the police and even worse, Isabelle and her sister Rebecca were standing there waiting with belts in their hands to welcome them back.

They had already had a cousin killed by a train and George had a friend who was electrocuted while climbing a train tussle. The boys' train hopping was a very dangerous thing, so the moms made sure this whipping was a memorable one. Rebecca tried to accept responsibility for Jimmy's part. She said he was the older of the two, and he should have known better. Isabelle insisted that it was George. He had been playing in that train yard for quite some time and regardless of how many times he got a spanking for it, he just kept going back. Trains would often hook up or drop train cars in that area and several kids had gotten hurt there, and three had died over the years. There were No Trespassing signs and a barbed wire fence, but that only added a challenge making George want to go there even more.

George got along quite well with his cousin and so did their moms. Their moms talked a lot about what happened after their parents had died. Rebecca was the youngest; the one who a family back near the old homeplace took in as a seven-year-old. She then, after many years, told Isabelle what happened to her as a girl. The man sexually abused her consistently until one day when she was about thirteen she became pregnant. They gave her baby away for adoption. Then by fourteen they had gotten in touch with one of her older sisters in Tennessee and they sent Rebecca to live with her.

She had married a man in Tennessee shortly after she had turned fifteen and had four girls. Then in late 1955, her husband died. After a while she got lonely, ended up with Jimmy and had no daddy to show for it. Since then she had been battling with her troubled child. Isabelle felt sorry for her and the two of them could actually relate to one another. Isabelle wanted her to stay longer, but she had her girls and now a grandbaby back home and Jimmy was to start school in just a couple days, so her visit was over.

Sometime afterward, maybe only two or three months later, her sister's oldest daughter called Isabelle; it was a real heartbreaking call. Jimmy, at just ten years old, was dead. He had tried to hop a train and slipped under it. His mother, Rebecca, had a nervous breakdown and was in the hospital in critical condition; not expected to live much longer. She had taken several pills; they pumped her stomach but the damage was thought to be too much for her heart. The next day her baby sister was also dead.

Isabelle made it a point to make sure that George attended these two funerals with her. She had told him, "This is your fault and you need to see what you caused." George did not really take this to heart. He felt no blame. He and his cousin did have a lot of fun and he was sorry he was dead, but he did not make him jump the train. And it wasn't his fault his aunt took too much dope.

By this time, George had already developed the "stuff happens" attitude and this was just a couple more funerals. Although he shook it off as no different from the many others he had been to, it really was a sobering moment for him to stand over his cousin's closed casket.

Although he didn't cry, his smart mouth and attitude both were quieted for several days.

They both talked to the psychologist about this on several occasions, pretty much as they did about all the other junks. George told him his mom was just going to blame him for her sister's and his cousin's death. Isabelle could only cry in fear that George would be next. The psychologist suggested to her that she should never speak of the ordeal with George again, and instead just go do something fun with him.

Isabelle tried to relate to George and make a connection with his aggressions and his sense of adventure. She was very scared for him but did not know what to do. However, she time and again proved to be creative and very spontaneous with her ideas. She would have him work in the garden with her and once they were gathering tomatoes and George complained that his hand had went through a rotten tomato and it stunk! Isabelle laughed and told George that when she was a girl they would have rotten tomato fights like a snowball fight and—incoming! Before George knew what happened, Isabelle had thrown a rotten tomato at George and it was on!

They had a lot of fun in the garden and her interactions with him in such ways kept a bond alive. George did love his mom very much and would later go on to recall so many more good and fun times with her. In fact his memory contains much more fun and good times with his mom than bad. They would go through phases of such times that bonded them. When he was in the mood to play games, she played checkers and dominoes with him for hours on end.

She not only was great at telling stories from her childhood, but also she took him fishing, hunting, and camping. But it was her who had taught him to ride a bike, catch a ball, and how to swing a bat. It was her who taught him how to shoot his first gun, how to cast his first rod and reel, and how to clean his first fish. All the things that a dad was supposed to do, his mother ended up doing. He found some resentment toward her even though he had fun just because of the fact that she was not his dad.

Some additional resentment toward her was fueled by the cruelty of other children when they learned more about his mom. For his second grade show-and-tell day in a big city school, George brings a raccoon tail and tells the story of the big coon hunt he and his mom had went on. A ten-year-old who is still in the second grade telling about the camping and fishing trip with only his mom. He told these things to other children who had dads and to those who had not failed any grades. Everything good or exciting he could come up with was from his mom. He simply resented her for this because he wanted it to be from his dad. To the adults around him, this had little justification or logic, but it did to him. Her disciplinary tactics to embarrass him did not help matters either.

He was always getting into some mischief or petty legal trouble, regardless of how hard or frequently she whipped him. She would preach her words of wisdom and threats that he would pay for doing wrong. He would be shoplifting while they were in the store, then later at home he would show off whatever it was, knowing it would get him into trouble. This got so bad that she would near strip search him before they left the store. It was always something stupid, just to show he could do it.

He would prowl the neighborhood, and for no apparent reason, break someone's car windows. He would go down the alley and set fires into trash cans just to get the fire department out. If someone left a bike out, it was gone. His mom would drag him if she had to, but he would take the bike back and tell them he was sorry. It just did not matter, he was always bringing home another stolen bike and she was dragging him again even by his hair if necessary to return the bike. But when the opportunity presented itself again he would just steal another one. His dad had been promising to get him another bike for three years, and he would always keep telling him he would, just wait and see. He had long lost faith in his dad getting that bike. Isabelle wanted to get him a bike so bad, but there was never enough money for it.

6

Ten Going on Twenty

A few weeks after turning ten, he had wanted the bike for his birthday that his dad promised he would get him, but did not. His mom could not afford it, so he was forced to just watch some of the other children ride the bikes their dads gave them. *Like heck*, he would think of a way to get another one.

This time, he thought he would outsmart his mom. He and one of his friends came up with a plan. They thought they had the perfect plan and rehearsed it till they had it down pat. George told his mom that his friend Joe had gotten two bikes for his birthday. His mom said that if George would work a couple days on the weekends to help her clean out their shed that he could have one of the bikes. Meanwhile Joe told his mom pretty much the same lie. It was late February, and was exceptionally warm and nice for that time of year, and for some reason, the moms bought the whole spring cleaning thing. His little brother did not have a clue, so he was not going to rat him out. Besides he had a bike their dad got him for being a good boy and she wanted to get one for George but could not.

George and Joe had already stolen two nice bikes, and now George got to ride for two days without answering a lot of questions about where he had been. Now it was time to go back home for him to show off the new bike to his mom, accompanied by Joe to confirm that it was for the work George had done. Wow, it worked; he actually pulled this one off. For better than a month, he enjoyed that bike.

One day Isabelle ran into Joe's mom at the store and began to thank her for letting George work for the bike. To Isabelle's surprise, she also had wanted to thank her for letting Joe work off the bike that he had. While these two moms came up with a plan of their own; they pretended to not know and just seemed to let it go. Joe's mom helped Isabelle plan a birthday party in the park for Fred that March. The moms had the boys invite all their friends, and parents too. It was going to be a big ice cream and cake party.

The two mothers stood together and got everyone's attention and called the two culprits forward as if to give them a prize or something. The moms then held the boys by the arms and from nowhere, two police officers rolled the bikes out in front of the boys and the mothers asked if any of the parents could identify the bikes, and they did. The mothers then dropped the two boys' pants in front of everyone there and bare-butt spanked the boys. In addition, the two of them had to apologize for the deed, and then get the usual talking to by the officers. George could never again recall getting one over on his mom quite this way. It was not that he did not continue to try, it was just that she had become quite hip to his sneaky ways.

School was finally out, but the summer vacation after the second time in the second grade was going to be on the streets with the neighborhood friends. Having spent two years in the first grade and now two years in the second, he is now required to go to summer school before he could go to school next year. This was to be his push toward readying him for the third grade. This was a joke, he did nothing productive here, if and when he showed up. Before the summer classes were over, he was expelled for fighting. He really had some behavior issues that no one seem to have the capabilities to address.

This summer his mom had little money and struggled for even the necessities, so there would certainly be no vacation trips. Besides, his uncle John had gone to

Florida to visit his son this summer, so he could not go there. Isabelle feared his boredom would get him into some bad trouble. This summer would not be all bad, they would play and do things that normal kids would do such as hide-and-seek in the dark, or play ball and such. In these things George and his brother had a lot of fun. There was always some kind of mischief also. His little brother was left out of most of these things because he would likely tell.

Isabelle would always tell the boys that the fun things of this world were often just a set up to draw them away from doing right. Most boys were adventurists at heart, but these boys were especially captivated by the forbidden, such as playing around the train yards, the viaducts, trusses, and even aboard the vacated train cars. On more than one occasion they took a wagon and loaded it up with rocks and pulled it up a viaduct to await one of the frequently passing trains; one that was carrying new cars from an auto plant. They would throw the rocks as a game into the windshields of the passing cars and trucks on the train. Back then the top of the train car was often totally exposed and sometimes even the sides and they had a blast taking advantage of that.

On a less-destructive-but-more-dangerous note, in the heat of summer, they often would take to playing under the viaducts. They went there because it was often cooler and they would paint graffiti on the walls, the columns, and on the upper support beams, as well as on any sitting train cars. They did this a lot. They never thought it hurt anything and some of the boys were quite talented and it was pretty safe. Oh sure, occasionally one of them would scrape a knee or something but that was about all.

This time was going to prove to be different. George was still only ten years old and was with about seven other kids, all just a bit, but not much older than him. One of the boys had climbed up under the viaduct to paint something up high and then a train was coming down the rail under him. The others yelled to hang on. He yelled back that he was good and as the train approached pigeons flew out and he fell.

George did not know what happened; he had yelled, he was good. They all scattered at the screech of the engine's breaks. George thought he had died for sure, but for some reason when he fell he landed on the other side of the tracks. It was probably a thirty-foot fall. He had for sure broken one of his legs. The bone was hanging out of it and he was hurting all over. Three of the other boys who had scattered to that side of the train quickly got him out of there before the railroad men made it back to them.

Boy, were they ever feeling a bit less adventurous for a few days. They were being told that he may never walk again. This was Joe, the boy who got the spanking with George for the stolen bikes earlier. *How could this be?* George wondered. He had perhaps been one of his best bike-riding friends and now he cannot ride bikes anymore. George recalled that the last year they once tied a rope on a stopped city bus and when it took off they went for a ride on a bike for about a block before they let go of the rope. Now his bike-riding pal will likely never ride again.

After a few days, George and one other went back and climbed up under the viaduct and finished the painting for him. They painted his name up there in red on a blue stripe and surrounded it with white stars as if to dedicate it to Evel Knievel himself. Inner city kids usually did not have much to give but they often had a heart for each other. George took a Polaroid picture of it and all the boys who had been there that day signed the picture and then took it to the hospital for him as a card. He had surgery; his hip had also been broken, and now he was in a body cast. After this Isabelle spanked George for his involvement. She would once again share her wisdom: when you disobey, the things that start like fun one way or another end badly, so it is your own fault.

Shortly after this, his uncle John came back early from visiting his son and stopped in to visit them. There was still better than a week before school was to start, so he persuaded Isabelle to bring the boys and spend a week on the farm. George was excited because his mom had told about a big gun that she used to go deer hunting with and how good of a shot she was. George knew she was a good shot because they had visited the farm before when she taught him how to shoot a .22. She could shoot tin cans superb with it, but a big gun— he wanted to see that.

This was a fun week, and George was little problem to anyone during this time. He learned that his mom really was a great shot. He seen his mom shoot an apple from nearly a football field away. No joke! This was with a .30-06 bolt action with a big scope. George wanted to try it but she said no and he started to get mad at her. His uncle John quickly pulled him aside and winked at him, giving him the shush finger over his mouth. He took him aside and told him if he did not give his mom a fit about it when he came back next time without her he would maybe let him shoot it. Isabelle only wanted him to shoot the .22 and she had no idea that John had let him shoot anything else, at least as far as George knew.

Well with another summer gone it was back to school for the boys. Immediately this meant they were back to more problems. Now at ten and a half years old he was placed into the third grade. The teachers soon started expressing concerns that he was just overpowering the other children and was proving to be quite uncontrollable. The thing many educators and psychologists were attempting to figure out is why George was as he was.

His older brother finally drifts back through in October. He has been expecting some great souvenir from the Woodstock concert. His brother was so messed up that he had forgotten he even had a little brother. George was so mad that he took his older brother's Stan Musial baseball and threw it in the trash! He no longer even wanted to be around his older brother.

This was also a prosperous time for medical experimentation as to what made the mind work. Isabelle had a state aid medical card, which meant that any and all medical bills were guaranteed to be paid. This was quite the meal ticket for some doctors. It would seem that all the money doctors could want was there for tests. They found George to be quite the profitable pincushion. His little brother showed no signs of similar issues; he was not a problem child at all, so there was no need to make a guinea pig out of him.

His mother's side of the family had a history of a rare and incurable nervous disorder—chorea or Huntington's disease. It is an incurable disease even to this day. It is genetically inherited and has several outward signs comparable to Parkinson's disease. This disease usually produces no visible symptoms until around age thirty.

However, members of George's family had manifested symptoms much younger, some before twenty years old. This disease was thought to have killed one of his grandparents. He had four uncles, three aunts, and nine of his cousins who have developed the disease. Over the course of twenty-five years after developing the treacherous disease, it killed them off one by one, with George being told this was also to be his fate.

There was a high demand for research surrounding this disease because no known research produced any positive results. They convinced Isabelle that George may be showing early signs and wanted to run tests. With the green light from her, virtually every type of doctor who could dip into the well of the medical card money just had to find out if this was causing George's behavioral problems. They tested the entire nervous system, from brain scans to spinal taps.

This included George trying many types of experimental drugs, as well as trying other forms of treatments. Such testing was added to the ongoing psychological research. This would include everything from hypnosis to shock treatments. However, at the end of months and months of experiments, all they would ever conclude is that they needed to run further tests. Therefore, they could get more money. Oh, but of course this was all for the advancement of medicine!

With the medical doctors never actually finding anything wrong with George that explained his behavior problem, and the psychologist, in place of providing a clinical explanation would frequently acknowledge that George was exceptionally bright. The judge, the teachers, the police officers, and her pastor, had repeatedly assured Isabelle that George just needed a good spanking. They could see that he had a well-behaved little brother. George just needed a good whipping, that's all!

What about his alcohol and street drug use at this time? He did use both but he was prescribed much more legal mood-altering substances during this time than his street use. As for his bad grades and how much he was kicked out of school, he was actually out of school more for medical experiments during a three-year period than he was for being kicked out. Combine his absence with the drugs he was prescribed, how could he really be expected to learn or act normal?

The teachers frequently give him swats with a paddle (with Isabelle's blessings) which would turn his bottom black and blue. The swats would occasionally go to the back of his legs as well making it difficult to walk, let alone run. Then when he would not want to run in PE class, he would get more swats with the paddle. The bruises always seem to still be there the next time he got swats, they seldom went away during the school year.

Isabelle tried her best, but her methods of discipline were never enough. She knew George needed a man to deal with him, but she could not provide one. Therefore, she began to think that she just needed to whip him as a man would. It was her job to raise him right and she was determined to even if it killed her, or him!

Then the newspapers showed pictures of yet another train derailment in the area. This was a big one. The whole train fascination with George was such a frightening one to Isabelle. She just started whipping George for no reason. She then told him she knew he somehow caused it. He thought she had completely gone off her rocker because he was with her when it happened. He had never even been to where that train derailed. She accused him of putting a penny on the track causing it to derail. He thought she had actually gone nutty as a fruitcake this time. The fact was that George knew a penny on a track wouldn't derail a train anyway, because he had tried it several times.

This was in the later part of the Vietnam era for the United States. The war stories filled the news and captivated much of the older generation, but to the youth this was a time of peace not war. The youth of this area rebelled in protests refusing to conform. These times brought cult movements of every sort—free love and the height of psychedelic drugs. Between his older brother and his druggy friends averaging twelve to fifteen years older and George's choice peers averaging six to nine years older than him, in this environment the drugs loudly called out to George. When his older brother was home he would give George cigarettes, or a hit off a joint or some form of alcohol to drink. Both brothers knew that their younger brother would tell so they left him out of this part. Other than for brief times in a week or two spurts, Marty was mostly gone.

Throughout the past few years to his ongoing treatment, the psychologist would prescribe various drugs, and some were quite strong. He often would go to multiple psychologists over a short time. One from the stress unit at the hospital, one with his mom, and one appointed by a court. Or perhaps he wouldn't like one and refuse to return to him and his mom would find another. As strange as this sounds they all prescribed a different medication for him.

When they knew of other medications he was on, they may have told his mom to discontinue some, but she seldom to never did. She felt that would be wasteful. If one doctor told her a pill was for him staying up too late, and another told her not to give him that anymore, she would still give it to him if he stayed up too late. Isabelle had been told by one he suffered an obsessive-compulsive disorder, another he suffered from depression; another said it was an anxiety issue; wait he is just hyperactive; yet another said he is so smart he is only acting up to get attention!

They would prescribe stimulant drugs, mood-stabilizing drugs, antianxiety drugs, and an array of antidepressants. Oh yes, let's not forget to include muscle-relaxing drugs from the medical doctors who were still trying to figure out if he contracted Huntington's disease. It really would not be until after 1970, until there was a standard medication treatment for ADHD and none during this time had actually diagnosed him with this. He was prescribed both uppers and downers at the same time, not to mention his drinking alcohol. The fact was he was not only suffering the effects of his home environment but also was also being victimized by their professional stupidity!

George quickly learned that if he did not like what they prescribed, he could sell or trade whatever he had for something that he liked, especially within his older brother's peers. Ironically, the system paid for them via the medical card. This made him particularly popular with older peers, and he did not have to fight as much as he had been to gain this popularity.

It was also necessary for his mom to get assistance from the state, in cash and for food. It was food stamps in a booklet for the food. The stamps were adequate, especially when she could grow part of their food. Often the need for cash would exceed the need for food. For these times, someone was always available to trade cash for the stamps. If his mom was short on paying the rent, one of the deacons from her church would give her twenty-five cents on the dollar. Of course this was only just to help her. In addition, George begins to steal the stamps from her purse and do some bartering of his own.

This had many other costs for George, it promoted the attraction of older peers toward him. Combine his rebellion at virtually any authority, especially his bitter disregard for the law, with his desire to fit in with the tough guys and with his drugs a motive for the tough guys to be there and you have a criminal mold. With him being too young to be prosecuted as an adult for carrying drugs, guns, or stolen goods, his older friends could find many uses for him. When he would get caught, he could say he found it. Or he would make up a story and point to someone he did not like, such as another police officer and say that he gave it to him to deliver somewhere.

The worst-case scenario was if he was arrested. He could act as a disturbed child. They would place him in the local stress unit. The shrinks would send him home with more drugs, while they receive their high-priced fees from more tax dollars! Beautiful, this kid could become a politician brilliantly working the system like this.

However, George became addicted to not only drugs but also the attention this would gain, as well as to the whole party scene. His preferred diet was to have barbiturates and booze by night and amphetamines by day. Days at a time slowly began to just vanish from the calendar. This must have given the illusion that this was the way to run from a bad childhood. However, taking these trips without ever leaving was always realized whenever he did come down.

Occasionally his dad would come by and give the boys five dollars once in a while. Usually, every other weekend, they would go a few blocks from their house to the bar where he would be. He would usually give them a few bucks. But there was a few times that there was a carnival near, and he would ask them to meet him there but he would never show up. He would tell them to come see him next week at the dime store and he would buy them something, but he would seldom even show up, then he would say money was too tight to waist on toys.

But then he had told George to come by himself and just the two of them would go to the show. George met him and they watched *Patton* with George C. Scott. Well at least George got to see it. His dad slept through the whole thing. He was so drunk and when it was over

George left him there sleeping. George also left with his dad's wallet.

This was during a time that George should have been enjoying an ordinary childhood. He did have more going for him than many children of future generations. Although they were poverty-stricken, fun things were still made available. George, years later, would never recall having a TV growing up until he was about ten. Then the family TV was a twelve-inch black and white. They would not have a stereo in the home until his eleventh Christmas, when he and his younger brother both received a small nine-volt transistor radio. They would tune them to be on the same station, separate them, and "wow," they had a stereo!

This was generally a much simpler time, and in those days, it was much more family oriented before the solitude created by children having a private TV. Back then if a household in the inner city even had one phone it was likely to be a party line, unlike now even small children have their own cell phone. A game for two was often checkers; a game for four was more likely to be dominoes or Chinese checkers. The basketball court was dirt and with but one basket; the backboard was a piece of wood mounted on a tree.

To spite his troublesome ways, there were many hugs from his mom, and she constantly told him she loved him. He and his little brother do things together, but George wanted to be an older person, not a little boy. He probably would have spent more time with him if he wasn't so quick to tell on him. This was odd. There were some things he had never told on George, like about the sex junk; but if he saw George steal a pack of gum in the store, he told.

This seclusion had an effect on his little brother as he started wanting to be more like George. During spurts of this they would have a lot of fun, and in spite of the animosity between them, they were actually bonded pretty tightly. George, in his own way, really loved his little brother. That was of course when he wasn't telling on him! They were the best of checker buddies, and no two brothers could build a bigger or better snowman together.

One of the most popular games was bottle caps. This was like softball, but the pitcher flipped a bottle cap to the batter and the batter used a broomstick as a bat. With such a simple life, why was it so complicated for George? His mom loved him very much and George loved his mom more than anyone else. He was just so angry and did not understand why. His little brother was not so upset, why was George?

Isabelle's disciplining had progressed from spankings to beatings by the time he was six years old. The beatings went from a paddle to a belt, then from his bottom end to his back. The "tools" went from the belt to an old-fashioned tree switch by seven. After all, the Bible and her preacher said that the rod was for the fool's back and she should not spare it, so she would use a switch on his back. In fact, according to the way she was taught, it was a sin for her to spare the rod. This action was only for George though, because his little brother did not do anything wrong. He was an angel.

By the time he was between eight and nine years old, the switch was to become an extension cord. At last a weapon that could bring blood through jeans. Lastly, before he would see his eleventh birthday, she had resorted to her fists. Sometime while he was still eleven years old she introduced him to Ms. Sweetie, the iron skillet that was given to her years earlier. She would use it as a paddle and give him swats like they did at school. She had previously used a wooden paddle, but had broken it on him. But Ms. Sweetie would not break. In this time era, the term "abusive parent" was not well-publicized or understood in the lower-class communities. In fact, many of the self-righteous middle class or upper class—the educated folks—often encouraged it to the parents of such a boy from the *hood*, or they would say he will become one.

Once, Isabelle was looking at George disgusted and said, "You make me crazy," with her fists tightly gripping her own hair. She punched him in both eyes with her hands full of her own hair. She then called the police and had them take the boy with two black eyes away to the stress unit. They had tried everything and nothing worked. Everything from placing him in a cell now and then, to even having one of the police dogs in an attack mode to try to scare him.

Some of the police officers had even taken a belt and spanked him several times. About the time he was eleven years old, they started slapping George around for cussing out his mother, then take him back home or to the psycho ward at the hospital, where he had already become a frequent visitor.

The teachers, the police, her pastor, and the psychologist basically said, "You go, girl!" The social worker would only suggest more visits to the shrinks, which in turn would only prescribe more drugs for George and for Isabelle. Did they ever consider the drugs as part of the problem? Evidently they did not or it was that their profit overran concern, because the drugs kept coming in stronger doses and in a much wider variety.

All of the combined circumstances in his life assisted in what would become his deepest addiction yet—sex. His aunt Anna had sexually educated him by five years old and then had intercourse with him some time before he was nine. She went on to encourage him to have sex with the daughter of her lesbian friend, while she and her girlfriend watched. Yes, the girl's own mother watched; the girl was around twelve.

Before George was ten he would have been with four different girls, three of them on numerous occasions. Now at eleven years old, this was one of his favorite highs. He wanted sex and it was not going to be with boys. Pornography was not going to quench this thirst. His older brother's porn stash only seemed to magnify the cravings of this young sex-crazed child. Some drugs he had taken must have been like an early form of Viagra, because he was on the prowl!

Isabelle continued forcing George to go to church. However, George did not think it was all bad, because the preacher's daughter had a crush on him. This girl had it so bad that George could get her to do anything. They would skip school together and do all sorts of other wrong things. George had her shoplifting and stealing anything and everything, especially from her dad and the church.

One Sunday morning, the pastor grabbed George by the arm and looked at what he thought was his watch. George replied, "Not a chance, preacher man, one of my babes got that for my birthday!" The preacher stood there looking at his daughter, and man, could she lie. However, it would not hold up, because the preacher's wife had his name put on the back of the watch at the jewelry store. At eleven years old, this ended George's visits to the Baptist church. Isabelle was too ashamed to make him go to church anymore. George could honestly say that he made a preacher cuss that day.

7

Out of Control

George's pain tolerance had increased so much by the drugs and by the frequency of the physical abuse that no beatings were ever enough to get him even to say ouch, let alone make him cry. Anger had boiled into a bitter hatred for life, which compulsively enraged him. This too was only enhanced by the drugs. If anyone knew or recognized the problems then they must have just looked the other way because none cared enough to intervene.

God certainly did nothing to help him, or so he felt and he was left to feel entirely forsaken and unloved. If there was a god, he was sure that He was not a god of love. George wanted nothing to do with any talk of love. He neither felt it, nor believed in it!

His experiences of the cruelty from the adults in his life only contributed to his own cruelty. Eventually it got to a point that even the teachers and the principal just left him alone, lest their cars could be burnt or their windows broken out, or tires sliced. Eventually they asked his mother to just keep him home.

This ended his the third-grade experience at this school. He was permanently expelled from yet another school in the middle of the school year. His vindictive ways had truly become a force to be feared; often leaving no evidence, only a suspicion that he did the deed. He was cold and cruel, just downright mean and by this point had learned to be brilliantly sneaky enough to get away with his stunts. As time went on, him getting permanently expelled from a total of three different schools forced them to move from this area to another to get George into another school.

His cruelty was often expressed toward animals. George was not loved, so why should they be? There appeared to be no end to what he would do to animals. Once George choked a cat; with it frantically clawing him, he just looked at its eyes until the cat was finally lifeless. George actually needed a few stitches after this one, but it wasn't going to cause this to be his last cat.

He had developed his own death claw into a throat and would not let go of an animal until it was dead.

He did not care how badly scratched he got, or if he got bitten. George often would be so high that he could hardly feel the pain anyway. However, he seemed to have a preference of choking dogs to death. He would jump a fence and face a dog coming at him with no regards or fear of being bitten and just squeeze until the movement was gone! He was responsible for an unknown number of animal killings and some were much more brutal or bloody—with an ax or a hammer and gardening tools.

It had been an array of similar cruelty that was now forcing them to move to yet another school district to finish the year out or the state truancy officer would remove George. Isabelle was partially split with this. She was often tempted to just let them take him, but she loved and wanted her son and was willing to keep trying. She quickly got him into another school, but it was not but a week later that a problem came up.

George's little brother would tell on him if he knew of anything that could get him in trouble. He was like Isabelle's extra set of eyes. She would reward him for telling and beat George. Then George would get even. This time George had been beaten up by another kid one day. He took an ice pick to school in his jacket the next day. However, before he could pull it, the teachers grabbed him and took it. George's little brother had ratted him out again! Not only did George get swats and expelled for another week but also his mommy also lit him up.

Then George decided to get some bricks and threw them up on their roof. He then climbed on their roof and waited for his little brother to come out then threw them at him. Then his mommy lit him up again. Fortunately, he never actually hit Fred with the bricks, but he sure did try.

As part of a revenge plan, George was good for a few days, to take suspicion off himself. Then late one evening, George took his little brother's cute little puppy dog, tied it to a heavy rock, carried it to a darkened spot on a busy street, and left it. Leading little brother to think the poor puppy had run off and was lost. The next morning George was willing to go looking for the puppy with his little brother. That way he could make sure that his brother would be the one to find it dead. All their mom would ever know was that poor little brother came back with a bloodstained leash. While he cried, George laughed because they were now even.

This was at the end of another school year that George had failed. The next year this would place a twelve-and-a-half-year-old to start the fourth grade. Now facing another summer, Isabelle's brother John told her that he would take him for the summer again. This time George was permitted to go on the bus by himself. His mom gave him twenty dollars as spending money and put him on the bus. The bus was due to drop him at a crossroad stop at 7:00 p.m. that same evening. It arrived a few minutes before and his uncle was not there. He told the bus driver it was okay his uncle would be there soon, but he was not. There was no phone, and no one there.

An hour or so after the bus left he decides to just start walking lugging a near fifty-pound metal suitcase. It was nearly seventeen miles to the farm, but he remembered the way. It was down the road he was facing and then just down the road that went left, right before the river where his uncle and him would fish. As he walked for what was seemingly forever, he realized it was ever-growing darker and darker.

This city boy who was afraid of nothing now was feeling mighty nervous. The coyotes were howling, the owls were hooting, and he was beginning to hear things in the woods. At some point on this long dark walk, he stepped on a snake and was scared half to death. He drops the suitcase he had been lugging around and just started running. That was a pretty heavy load anyway; it had him stopping to rest quite often.

Now that it was nearing daylight he was able to see the road a bit better and he sees the bridge, then the drive entrance to the farm. At last he sighs with relief—the house. His uncle had breakfast on and told him he thought he was not coming until seven the next evening, as he set some food in front of George. *What a way to start a vacation*, George thought. His mom had told his uncle when to expect him, but he would often misunderstand things he read or was told. Aside from being nearly completely deaf, he could barely read.

His uncle John asked where his clothes were and George told him about the big snake he killed with his suitcase and that he just left it there because it must have had blood and snake brains on it. Sometime later that day he and his uncle walked down about two miles to get his suitcase. Right by the suitcase there laid a piece of rope that someone had lost. His uncle started laughing and said, "Here is the snake you killed," and they laughed most the way back to the farm. His uncle John told him that he too was afraid of something. This got George's attention because he did not think he was ever afraid of anything.

He had seen his uncle open a beehive barehanded without a head net or anything and gather the honey. He would get stung a few times, and in a few weeks, he may check the hive again. George would not openly admit to being scared, but he would not have done that because he was especially afraid of bees. He saw his uncle walk into a snake-infested pond to tie a rope around a cow that had gotten stuck and pull it out with the tractor.

There was no way George would have done that either; he would pick up a snake or kill one if he knew it was there and could see it, but this pond had several snakes in it that you couldn't see.

Once when George was feeding the pigs and hogs, a very fat sow, weighing over five hundred pounds, quickly charged at George, and his uncle jumped in front of it with a piece of 2 × 4 inch board and let that sow know he was the boss. Now he was telling George he had a fear. George was curious but he never would tell him. He just told him he was afraid to say! Ha ha! This drove George bananas and sometimes when he would ask he would say, "When you grow up I may tell you," and then just laugh. George really thought his uncle was the toughest man alive, even tougher than his dad but he said even he had a fear.

This was a very similar summer as his other one with a few changes. His uncle's house was finally finished, and he had a housekeeper three times a week. The housekeeper was the very girl George had hit it off with the first summer on the farm, and man had she ever changed. She was now well developed and was just getting ready to have her fourteenth birthday. He was thinking it was sure going to be a fun summer.

The summer progressed much as the other one had. Only this time he was not just shooting the .22 or 410's, it was the 20-gauge automatic, the 12-gauge pump, one of three 30-30s, the 7mm, 8mm, and 9mm. At his age, he probably had one of the rarest adventures with weaponry. He learned about history in a hands-on way without even thinking he was learning history.

His uncle was quite the collector. He had over two hundred guns. George got to hold some historic WWII weapons that were fixed to not fire. This included a .50-caliber Browning machine gun like his dad had told him was mounted on one of the trucks he had driven back in the war.

George also was privileged to fire some that still worked, such as an M1 carbine, and a Springfield sniper rifle. Indeed he had been learning a lot about guns at his uncle's, including how to handle them. His favorite was the very one he saw his mother shoot so well. It was that .30-06 bolt-action. It had a long barrel compared to several others and was very hefty. It had a scope on it that was dead set for a hundred yards. He was determined to match his mom's record with that gun.

She had placed five of five within a two-inch pattern. This was unrested, just aim and shoot. He used an awful lot of ammunition trying and had made his arms very sore from shooting it, but never could match it. The fact is, his best try was three of five that whole summer; but that would be in even hitting the paper plate that the two circle was drawn on, and he had rested it. Frankly he thought it was just too heavy. He wondered how she ever got good enough to do that.

In between the fishing and hunting trips with his uncle, there were the chores that made him the money to pay for all the ammunition. His uncle was not totally spoiling him; there was plenty of hard work to do. George had to feed the chickens, the hogs, the cattle, the cat, and the two dogs. He had to burn the trash and help go for the groceries. There were also the jobs of cleaning the fish, to twirling the head off each chicken they would eat; this process would include plucking the feathers off them as well. There was wood to stack, brush to burn, and so on. His uncle had a saying, "when the work is done it's time for fun!"

The neighbor girl and him did get together but not nearly as much as he thought they would, not more than eight or ten times over this summer vacation. His uncle kept him too busy to get with her very much. Now with another summer gone it was time to go back home.

About this time his older brother Marty, after six years in la-la land, drifts back through. He had a car and drove down to pick George up. This was a quiet ride home; his brother did not want to talk and did not want George to talk. They just smoked some weed and listened to some music.

He only stayed at home a short while until he got a job and then moved out. Shortly after he moved out this time, he got married. Perhaps the generation gap was just too large between them, but he and George frankly were never that close anyway. But this also left George with more bitterness, because deep down inside he wanted his brother to stay, simply because he wanted a big brother.

George would have had more to do with his little brother as well if he did not suck up to mommy so much! He also would have liked more friends as well, but the only way he could seem to gain any popularity with his school peers was by becoming the toughest one of the bunch.

When he was in the fourth grade, he broke his hand in thirteen different places on a boy's head, and within a couple of weeks, literally busted the cast over the same boy's head. George often picked fights that he knew he could not win, just to build a reputation as a crazy person. Honestly, just to make people leave him alone. Much of it wasn't to get attention as presumed; he really just wanted to withdraw into his little world.

He once bit a hole out of the shoulder of another boy and removed part of another's ear. Through his adolescent years, George suffered at least some twenty-two broken bones, multiple black eyes and bloody noses, was stabbed three different times (once with an ink pen driven into his arm, a lead pencil into his wrist, and an unknown sharp metal object into his lower back). And yes, he had quite a few trips to the dentist as well.

He would fight as mean and dirty as he could. If someone were too tough for a face-to-face fight, they would get it unexpectedly from behind. One way or another, if he had it in for you, you could depend on getting it. The local sports club had a program to accept low-income boys for judo and karate classes. This program potentially could have offered a way up, because he liked it, and they insisted upon self-discipline. But for nearly a year and a half, while they collected money from some fund, its instructors only better equipped George with the ability to be more competitive and defend through a better offense! Of course he was well-behaved around his instructors, following instructions, being attentive and obedient while in their presence. He then would take what he learned and put it to the test on the streets.

Another contributing factor to his rage was—in George's eyes—his mother's fault. With Isabelle having been a seamstress by trade when she worked, combined with the fact that she had very little money, she would often make the boy's clothes. Although she was quite good, the trend for a nearing-teenage boy in this time area was to wear blue jeans, not corduroys, and plain colors, not striped or checkered-patterned pants. This was now the early part of 1971, and these styles and colors were now considered nerdy, unlike what she had learned to be cool in the fifties for his older brother. This was no longer the days of sock hops; it was the hard rock and country music era. With the natural cruelty of children George would be picked on or teased by other children for wearing 1950's clothes. It took little of this and he would boil over with rage and just could not take it anymore. Somewhere between ages eleven and twelve he proved to have zero tolerance for anyone who teased him, and after he was twelve, at all cost he would get even from then on.

Being much tougher than many his own age, he could have controlled most of the teasing, however he sought to hang out with much older peers. Many of them could whip him and had made a habit of picking on his clothes. But just because they were able to beat him up, it never stopped him from trying to get them for it.

Not only would he violently explode toward those who had teased him but also it progressed to where if someone even looked at him wrongly he was likely to go off on them. He just would no longer wear any of the things his mother made for him. He would rebel and throw a rageful tantrum-like episode at the sheer mention of homemade clothes. He would literally destroy the inside of the house, breaking the windows or doors. He took a butcher knife to their couch and kicked the table legs out from under the coffee table. He threw a lamp through the living room window. All this to protest the homemade clothes. He just was not going to wear that stuff. He demanded no less than store-bought jeans and T-shirts.

This was taking place in a time when his tolerance to virtually all others had already become so short-fused, with enraged and spontaneous eruptions, especially toward his mom. She was so distraught with this and eventually felt that she had no choice and would sacrifice many other things to provide such for him. The need for money for such became a motive for further permitting the children to go around Otto, because he would, in turn, occasionally give her a few dollars for support.

Once during a visit to see their dad, their dad started a fight with a black man. Their dad wasn't prejudice by no means; this was over the supreme court's unanimous decision to reverse the conviction of Muhammad Ali for refusing to serve in the army. Otto was calling him a scum, not worthy of living, saying he would cut his throat if he could get close enough to him. The other man began defending Ali's rights, and Otto went into attack mode. The bartender sent the boys out the back door and told them to go home because the police were coming. They waited to go home, watching from a distance until after seeing the police take their dad away. They never even told their mom about this one.

About this time, Isabelle had been writing one of her sisters in California. Her niece and her husband had lived near the big earthquake of 1971, and they wanted to move. She welcomed them to come stay with them, and they did. George had never met his cousin. She was much older than him, around twenty-two years old then. Her husband was probably in his thirties, and George just stayed clear of them. All they wanted to do was talk about the earthquake and that only held George's attention for a bit. It wasn't more than a few days and George had embarrassed his mom so much she just had him put in the stress center. By the time he was out, they were gone. Such stays in the hospital were almost always about a month long.

He had always seemed to get into fights in the past, but for some reason after this particular stay in the hospital, it worsened. Now it would seem that George was in a fight nearly every day. From very early in his school years, he had been beaten up a lot by other bullies and had started a lot of fights, but they weren't every day. He would get into a fight two or three times a month before this. He always faced the fight with guts. He would not run even when he knew he would lose a fight. By this time, he was actually becoming a reputable bully himself. Because of his age, his classmates posed little problems to him, but he didn't want to hang out with them and preferred to hang out with those his age or older. He had a much harder time with the older group and would get knocked around pretty good.

The only friends for him now were other troublemakers. In a large inner city school, he easily became one of the top three school bullies among his classmates. One thing that assisted this was the fact that he failed his classes. He was three years older than most in the fourth grade. This let him just walk on most anyone in his class.

What he learned was that it was just as lonely at the top as it was at the bottom. He certainly could not trust other thieving backstabbers. There were no real friendships for him here. Yes, he had what he called friends, but they also were like junior hoodlums. Although they may not tell on you for doing something bad, they would not quickly speak up for you if you were innocent either, and George understood that was not how a real friendship was supposed to be. He was lost and running aimlessly in circles. It seemed as if there was no place to mentally run where he could not see his own tail.

At one moment, he did not want to be alone; at another, he wanted to just be left alone. He wanted to be high or drunk, but then he hated being high or drunk. Surely in part, the sexual abuse he had underwent played a role, as did the religious confusion and the poor parenting. However, the prescription drugs should be credited with having played a large role in his behavior. Sure, drug and alcohol abuse was often said to be a factor, but only when talking about illegal drugs. The prescription drugs were never once referred to as a possible factor in any evaluation of causes for his behavior.

Then on one of the occasions that he was in a stress unit, his mother talked them into letting him come home early. In November 1971, his only living grandparent was about to die from cancer. Isabelle took George to see her. As he approached his grandma, she placed her rosary into his hands. She told him that was the one her mom used and gave her when she came to the States. She said that her mom knew she would never see her on this earth again, just as she knew this was her and George's last talk on earth together. This very frail but faithful Catholic then asked her Baptist daughter-in-law for her Protestant Bible. She then places it in George's hands and told him, "It will not matter if you choose to be a Catholic or a Baptist if you live like this book tells you to live. In this book are the instructions from God. It is the map to find Him."

Although the loss of his grandmother never pulled his emotions to a place of tears, this moved him enough that he made a secret treasure out of that Catholic rosary and that Protestant Bible. She began choking and the doctors and nurses asked them to step out. She never regained consciousness, and within a couple more days, she was gone. It stuck with him that she knew they would never speak again and that he was the last one who she actually spoke to. After her death, it appeared that for some reason he began to withdraw even more from people, and would not be talked to about God.

He was feeling cursed being an outcast and a loner, much like his dad had been. Death had become such a familiar ground. Not only had he lost his grandma but also he had attended countless funerals. Most of his aunts and uncles on both sides have all died by this time from this disease or from that one. He had lost the one cousin who was run over by the train. He lost three of his other cousins and some other friends of the family to the Vietnam War. He had a close relative who was murdered, a cousin who was shot by the police, another died in a knife fight in a bar, and there were four cases of suicide in his family.

If some sort of violence or a drug overdose did not kill off his friends, the law had taken them away. Some of his older friends were already in prison by this time. He knew it would eventually get everyone. It seemed a cold attitude. Remaining void of emotions was his only protection. Actually, from age ten onward, he would not shed a single tear.

The funerals he would attend would, more often than not, be dysfunctional. For example, George was chosen to be a pallbearer by his grandmother before she died, as were all the other pallbearers. When his dad came to the funeral, he was drunk and was thinking he would carry his mom. When he was told the grandsons were chosen, he began blowing out most of the candles that had been lit. His sister began yelling at him and he punched her in the face, breaking her nose and knocking over several of the flower arrangements, before he could be restrained by other family members and then removed by the police.

At another funeral, his uncle turned over his dead son's casket in anger toward his son for choosing to go into the army rather than priesthood! It was a common sight to see people show up to funerals drunk and most always afterward the drinking was the seeming tradition! This uncle (drunk) then drove his car head on into another car, killing himself and three others who were in the other car. What else could really be expected of George?

Now nearing thirteen and in the fourth grade, having been held back three times, he spent more scheduled school days either kicked out of school, skipping school, or being experimented on by doctors to being locked into a psych ward of some hospital (even into an actual state asylum). This place could be a story all of its own. A mixture of his rebellious attitude and his enraged hatred for authority figures fueled his vindictive ways and made him incapable of functioning in a productive way.

Once George was so mad at the school principal that he coaxed five of his wannabe friends to meet him after dark outside the principal's house, each with baseball bats. George brought a gas can and lighter. Within just seconds, every window and light on the principal's car was busted and it was on fire. The boys were long gone. Some time later, two of the boys were convicted for this crime, but George and the others were not even implicated.

This do-not-tell attitude was the honorable way of the streets, and the means of determining friends was often at the expense of one taking the rap for others! Even his little brother was finally learning this. Besides, revenge could come in drastic ways. A crowded school hallway had provided cover for some to get a pencil into the back if you were a snitch! This and other types of aggression were often without any evidence of who the aggressor was, even if others saw! You did not have to belong to any gang to be under this protection, or under a threat. This was not necessarily a gang-related way, it was just the way it was!

The psychologists just could not analyze George. They would conclude that he was more than capable of learning, but that he just would not. Once, the good doctor told Isabelle that George was so intelligent that he felt George may be pulling stunts just because he was bored. In spite of their educations, they were incapable of factoring in things like he had been drinking beer since before he was out of diapers.

George had smoked his first cigarette before he was six and his first joint was not far behind. By eight years old he was smoking a half pack of cigarettes a day. When his older brother was in town he would get him a stash. He thought that would keep the brat out of his stuff. He would steal or trade drugs for them; whatever it would take to get the smokes, he would do it. To top it off with drinking the booze and taking all the drugs the shrinks had prescribed, could he really be expected to focus on school? Intelligent? Maybe he could have learned if it was not for all the brain cell-destroying junk they pumped into him. Do parents even know that Ritalin is a little more than cocaine? And top this off with other drugs he was taking as well as the alcohol.

Some time before his thirteenth birthday, at the start of winter, he skips school and ran away and hitchhiked down to see his uncle in Missouri. He told him his mom said he could come see him. He thought he would perhaps stay there for a while to get with the neighbor girl again, but she had moved away, and there were no other girls for miles. So after a couple of days, his uncle put him on a bus back home, knowing he should have been in school. But on the way back, the bus stopped at the St. Louis bus terminal, and George got off because he wanted to see the arch. He remembered stories from there from his mom and older brother. For several weeks afterward, he just roamed around the St. Louis area.

In these weeks, he stole anything and everything he could just to survive the cold. As for drugs, he found that the homeless community had them too. If he could not steal something to trade for them, he could sell the drugs for a local pusher to get more for himself.

8

No End in Sight!

Finally, he is picked up by the police walking near a known dope house across the Mississippi into Illinois. He was wasted and did not remember much, but he was not actually in possession of any drugs and there was no known warrant on him. He told them he ran away because he was abused. So after a couple of days in the local juvenile holding, they placed him into a foster home. What a joke. He then split.

He had been gone for about two months total when he finally made it back to Indianapolis. As he was walking at night, a cop stopped him. He was obviously wasted in appearance, but this real issue was he was carrying a stolen *loaded* gun and nearly a half pound of weed. He told the police he found the gun with the dope and then told him he was suicidal, knowing where that would send him. He did not spend more than an hour in the cell before the paramedics came to take him to the mental health stress center.

George knew the charges for the drugs and gun could send him to the detention center for a good while, but if he opted out to be a mental space cadet, he could be out after a month or so with some follow-up treatment and he would be in the clear.

After the standard thirty days in the stress center, he was released back into his mom's custody. This of course was conditional upon him going back to school, and in him seeing yet another physiologist. For nearly three more months, he would be required to see this guy as part of the legal process. Otherwise they would bring him up on the charges.

In an in-depth attempt to analyze George, this head shrink took him to see a rated R movie for his thirteenth birthday. He was now a teenager. This was by far not his first such movie because he and some of the other boys would, on occasion, sneak into a drive-in. This was different though, because he just walked into the theater like the other adults.

This film was extremely violent and contained some nudity. This psychologist was evaluating his reactions to the scenes. Perhaps because his mother would never approve of George viewing such, this psychologist must have figured he, in turn, would create a male bond that George would hopefully be more likely to confide in.

This was somewhat effective, but not necessarily with the effects the psychologist anticipated. This bond briefly had the appearance of friendship and to a psychologist eager to accomplish his task. He then incorporated the cooperation of his wife. His wife was also a psychologist and began inviting George on family-like outings. Within just a few weeks of such outings, they made the mistake of occasionally inviting him into their own home.

Then once, with them unaware, George had unlocked a window to later return in their absence and steal a few items. He found the opportune moment, and as if with a rampage-type madness, he literally destroyed the inside of their house. He broke everything he thought they may have a personal attachment to. In a later and last session with this particular psychologist, George tells him he knows he had been nice only to figure him out and it was not going to work. Then George tells him with his standard wise-guy tone, that he heard it through the grapevine that he had been robbed! Looking as if he did it!

This man could not have proven anything. There was no physical evidence to convict George of this. However, just in case he was to try, George boldly threatened by telling him that if he was questioned about it, he would say that the man had molested him, or that he had him to do this so he could collect insurance. His good intentions to help George were repaid by the creation of turmoil for him and his wife. They had already lost a lot of sentimental things when George demolished the inside of their home, and knowing George's history, he just could not afford to call his bluff, so he lets it go silently.

This promoted some real arrogant thoughts in George, as well as confirmed to him that mental manipulation could be as profitable as stealing and that it was especially easy when your abilities are so underestimated. George was ever mentally growing and learning new games to play on those who thought he was mentally not right. Some of his future pranks indicated that he really wanted to be thought of as stupid or even crazy just so he would be underestimated. But to confound even himself, other times he intended to really pull off a fast one and he fails because he is not as smart as he thought and he belittles himself. Unrealized to him was, his attempts to show off his intelligence seem to fail because of drugs. He would often think of a brilliant plan and lose his thought in midstream, as if his mind would have a light go out.

Some of the prescription drugs had a dazing effect that, when he would overmedicate or when mixed with alcohol. It produced days of total memory loss or only faded memories as if they were dreams. Truth or reality to him could be whatever he imagined it to be. For a few months it was as if he would start what he thought was a brilliant scheme and have the plan all worked out and forget where the building or house was that he was planning to rob. Someone would make him mad, and he would plan out what he was going to do about it and forget who he was going to beat up or con out of some money.

The drugs and alcohol fogged so much. He may wake up in bed with some girl and no memory of who she was or how he got there. He once woke up with the memory of going to bed at home, to find three days had past and he was three states away. Another time he awoke remembering that he was flat broke and then finds a roll of cash in his pocket, with everything a blank. Regardless, he would somehow always end up back home. He would tell his mom it was her great cooking that kept him coming back and her mouth that kept him leaving.

He would frequently use all his drugs and he would steal or switch meds with his mom. He had found an over-the-counter sinus pill that resembled his mom's Valium. He also was prescribed the same ones, but after he took all of his, he would take hers, after switching them with the fakes. He thought he was slick. She never did catch on to this one. It only cost him a couple of bucks for a bottle of these pills that he switched for fifty 10-mg Valiums. If he didn't take them, he could certainly sell them or trade them for something he did want.

During this time, everyone seemed to know he would be running away after a week or so at home. He would be gone for two or three days at a time; sometimes for a week or longer. During the school season, he knew he couldn't stay gone to long, but most all weekends no one knew exactly where he would go. The police could not find him. But then Mondays he would just show back up at home; he would either be ready to go back to school for a few days, or to a stress unit for near thirty days.

Often he would come home in torn-up clothes or all beat up, or just plain filthy . This was a scary time for his mom. She was sick with worry all the time about where he had been. But this was often done with a clouded memory of where he had been, or he would tell such an unbelievable tale he would not be believed. He once told he went to California and had spent the week on the beach, but he had only been gone two days. But he really believed he went!

It seemed to others as if he was involved in every fight he could get into. This was probably one of the most violent times for him thus far. This would result in his involvement in some pretty violent incidents. Although he never killed anyone, it was not that he did not come close! These times also produced the losses of some of his would-be friends to overdose or as a result from their own violent ways. As time goes on, being gone for a day or so, became a week or so at a time.

Once while George was gone on one of his roaming journeys, his little brother had gotten jumped by one of his old friends. When George returned and found out, he was mad. No one was going to beat up his brother except him. He then picked a time and place that fit his plan for revenge. When he got him, he beat him just short of death. No one saw him except his little brother. He just left him lying facedown in the alley. The boy spent better than a week in the hospital and would require surgery even after he got out of the hospital. George had stomped his teeth in, severally damaged one of his eyes, and just kept kicking him in the ribs and back.

The boy told police that it was George, but when they questioned him, he insisted he had been right there in his yard with his brother playing ball ever since supper. When they asked Fred separately, he also said that he and George had been there playing all evening. Isabelle knew they were in the yard playing because they had been in and out. Although she could not account for their every minute, and she would not put it past George, but Fred would not lie to her, especially not to save George. The police officers also bought this one because they also had experienced Fred telling on George all the time. So no charges were brought up for this incident.

George and Fred worked together on this one. George had planned it all out. He had told the boy earlier that day that he knew of a shed at the end of his block that had some tools in it that they could steal and to meet him there at eight thirty that night. So that evening after supper, George and Fred asked their mom if they could play ball in the yard, she said, "Okay." This was normal. She would always let them go out and play if they were staying in the yard. Just before eight thirty, they both came in the house and asked their mom if she would make them a snack—some homemade pudding or something. She said, "Okay, come back inside in just a little while to get it while it is hot." As they went back out the door, George ran down the alley with a nightstick he had stolen from a cop.

Fred immediately started throwing the basketball against the backboard and was hollering and making the noises as if George was there and he was talking to him. About five minutes later, Fred sticks his head in the back door and hollers to his mom, "Is it done yet?" His mom replied, "In about five more minutes," and backed out hitting the backboard and making noise with the ball.

George then jumped over the fence back into the yard and Fred threw him the ball just before Isabelle stuck her head out the back door to tell them it was ready. The two of them went into the house as if nothing had happened. Fred always looked up to George after this as some kind of mastermind or something, and the two of them got along a lot better. But George would still turn on him at the slightest thought of him telling on him.

George was often entirely consumed by an untamable rage that would make him strike at anything, as if he were possessed by some demon. He would just be sitting quietly at the kitchen table waiting for the meal to be finished, and for no apparent reason, he would throw something across the kitchen. Or if during the meal he wanted some more mashed potatoes and his brother reached for them also, he may throw them all over the floor and scream at him, telling him to eat them off the floor like the dog he was. If they had a guest over he would act out with the intent to embarrass his mom.

He would continue refusing to conform to all forms of authority. Naturally, this was especially his mother. To say that he absolutely drove her bananas would be an understatement. After all, she had blamed him for everything that had ever gone wrong, or so poor George perceived. George would seldom go to school, or if he went, he would get kicked out shortly after.

In the year between thirteen years old and now, he was not at home with his mom and little brother more than sixty days total. During this time, he had become lost in the ways of the streets. His little brother had now begun to idolize him and would listen to the bad reports as if with envy. There were a couple of petty warrants for his arrest, not to mention that the truant officer was trying to get him, but he was becoming quite well at eluding captivity.

Then one day, just before he was to turn fourteen, he was really wasted. He was walking downtown by the courthouse, and for some reason, began urinating on the courthouse steps. He thought it was even funnier to try and wet on the officer that subdued him. This put an end to him eluding the police—he was finally caught. He later claimed to have absolutely no memory of doing this.

Contrary to many of the educator's opinions , George really did have the potential to be quite bright. His actual intelligence was misunderstood and often hidden by the overshadowing results of the drugs, or the emotional damage from his environment. Without calculating the contributing factors, any idiot could predict the same or worse future that the teachers made for George.

They told Isabelle, "He would never learn and would always be worthless!" Now from the testimony from teachers, the psychologist, and George's mother Isabelle, a judge said he believed George was criminally insane and would eventually do harm warranting his permanent removal from society! The judge ordered an extensive ninety-day evaluation to be done in a state facility. George, grasping the severity of his situation, begins to think of something.

This place was clearly not a stress unit or some wing or ward of a regular hospital. It was the Logansport State Hospital. It was for the really mentally ill. This place was full of the truly disturbed; having autism, mental retardation, schizophrenia; those with bipolar and such. This place was like a prison. It was securely locked down and he knew better than to do something to act up in there.

To the shock of many, he briefly behaved and was very cooperative. Within the three months in this state institution, George convinced a fresh team of psychologists that he was just an ordinary little boy who had just been abused and just needed love! He had been a victim and needed a chance. And with a consistent series of convincing lies, a different judge then ordered that he be placed back in foster care, with of course probation and entry into a special school. Ha! Free again. This time only to run away, and other than brief times was on his own until well after he was fifteen.

His mere survival from this point depended on his ability to manipulate or to control others to be in charge of the situation at hand. There would be no mentionable fifth through eighth grade, recalling only the school of the streets! Oh sure, he occasionally would briefly end up back at his mother's for part of a day here or there, or in a foster home here or there.

One such time, he ended up temporarily detained by the police in another city. He gave them the address of his old house that he knew had just been torn down and gave them a fake name. Then he told them he had run away from home because his dad beat him. He supposed that because he was such a great liar, they decided placing him in a temporary foster home, while they checked his story out. But before they figured out who he really was, he ran again. It appeared he was such a gifted liar that he could convince anyone of pretty much anything.

Foster care to him in the past was a lot like modern slavery. "Why?" was unknown. He never claimed that any foster parent had actually done him wrong. It was that he felt like he was owned. Whether for a day, or a week, he felt he was just their property or a way for them to collect money from the state. George just assumed this was a common feeling with other foster kids too. He wouldn't ever get too friendly with other foster children because he figured he would only be there a day or so. He would simply not give the foster system a chance. He felt no more stability in foster care than on the streets, so he just kept running. But to where?

George just drifts around the local area of home, until about the later part of May of 1973. He then starts hitchhiking out west. He stops in St. Louis to do some sightseeing. His mom and older brother had many stories about this city so he thought he would check it out. He knows he was in St. Louis back before he was thirteen, but his memory of it was so vague and it was cold out. Now it is summertime and he wants to see the party side of this city. There, he found some good times and some bad ones. At his last night there, he was wasted and had gotten beat up by a couple of black guys. He had never personally been called a honkey before this. He felt the insult by that was as bad as getting beat up. He promised himself to never go back to St. Louis.

He then changes his mind about going out west and hikes back home for a few days of mom's home cooking and Band-Aids. While he was home this time, his little brother went to a theater with him and one of his older friends to see *Messiah of Evil*. His friend worked at the theater and would sneak them in. Again little Fred told his mom and was she ever mad that they took his little brother to see such a movie. She started her preaching hellfire and brimstone. George gets mad, and before he leaves he tells her where to go.

He gets so wasted over the next few days, he was found one morning unconscious behind a local bar. They couldn't get him to come to, so he ended up at the hospital, and then into the stress unit again. It was now mid-June, and he was pretty strung out and it was a week or so before he remembered even being there. This time in there, he got to know the personal side to a hooker he had been with once in the past. She got out slightly before he did and they planned to hook up later. When he was released, his mom said she would take him in. He would no doubt have to go to court, so after a couple of days at his mom's, he then hooked up with this gal from the psych ward.

By late December of 1973, George had left her. He had gotten a case of the crabs from her, so he ran again. This had so far been the longest stay in one place for a long time. He had been with her for nearly six months. He had a supplier and ran dope out of her place when she was gone, making some money her way. Together they had quite a racket and he had never had so much cash or sex. Once he remembered counting over ten thousand dollars for a week's take, and the sex was not just with her. He sold drugs that attracted some of her girlfriends and he frequently ended up in some pretty strange settings.

Without too graphic of descriptions or without having personally experienced something similar one could not truly imagine this setting. This would include one or more acts of bestiality, bondage, and multiple partners. George never quite understood the full cause of his promiscuous lifestyle. He actually felt it was normal, or even prideful that he could be with so many adult women at his age.

Perhaps one could look for causes in insecurities or from the early sexual abuse. Either way, it would seem that being with adult women became a way that he could feel he was displaying or proving his manhood. He would be stoned or drunk at a party one night, and may wake up the next day, or even days later in an unknown town or house, in bed with someone he had little to no memory of.

The reality for George was that becoming a man would ultimately be the way to run from a childhood he did not want. This would prove to have lasting effects on others as well as on himself. His reputation alone caused damaging consequences. He was never to be trusted and would never have any close (real) friends, or family that would have him around, or at least not for very long.

During the times between his fourteenth birthday and now nearing fifteen, his criminal activities were more or less just the means of existence for him. No one seemed to care whether he slept with a prostitute or alone on a park bench. Whether he was freezing cold, sick, or starving. If he was not a bother to people, he did not exist to them. Happy, sad, or mad; whether he was drunk or sober, beat up, cut up, or just doped up, he really didn't think anyone cared.

He had been seeking adult women since he was twelve years old, and with drugs at his disposal—make no mistakes—he got them now. Now, with having experienced years of sexual abuse combined with his own misconduct would place many lifelong scars on George, as well as producing other victims as well! There should have been guilt and shame felt, but it was confused with a false sense of pride! There is nothing like the male ego on a sexual rampage. It had to be him who was going to be "all that" with the girls!

After about a month on the streets, George then moves in with a local palm reader who had also been a regular drug customer. They had been sexually involved a couple times before, but this time he moves in with her. She was around twenty-four years old and was a very dark person, having rooted practices in satanic rituals. She, of course, was a phony in her trade, being nothing more than a con artist. But in her real life, she really was dark and sought the father of darkness.

George had previously experimented with the dark powers, but only briefly. Now he finds himself becoming extensively involved and ever-fascinated with the supernatural powers that exist outside the Godhead; seeking a supernatural power, undergoing experiments in the practice of conjuring up the spirits of the dead in séances and through psychic powers.

Almost in a compulsive way, he began practicing various forms of magic, almost living in a fantasy world made of sorcery and voodoo. The Ouija board was nothing. He really wanted to meet Satan himself. Of course during this time he was virtually never straight; the drugs had a stronghold on him, especially the purple microdots (LSD). His memory of this time is very chopped up with little logic. He can't even recall how long he was with her, but it was said to be about three months. He, at some point, makes it back home and then his mom started saying he needed to go into the stress center for a few weeks, so he takes off again.

He really didn't believe anyone ever had cared about his future, let alone about him, but this just wasn't true. George had occasionally come across several different people who had briefly reached out to him, and many who had consistently tried. But the real thing was that he would not trust anyone. There was even one individual who was persistent over the years with kindness. Once when he was about ten or eleven, a neighboring handicapped churchgoing man tried to reach George with his kindness. George displayed so much cruelty and disrespect. He cussed him out and spat on his face. This man was a next-door neighbor at the time. He was very overweight and George would always call him names. He referred to him as a fat slob, as the super blob, or as a morbid freak of nature. As odd as it may seem, this guy never told George's mom. He would only tell George that Jesus loved him.

George thought that this guy was as crazy as him! He would persistently preach to George, and he would just cuss him out all the more or tell him he was crazy and he would preach all the more. This guy had to be a little nuts to put up with George, to just keep being kind to him was insane. This Jesus freak was lucky George never hurt him, but for whatever reason he didn't. Some thought that George was entertained by the conflict, but that wasn't it. George had not only gotten used to him but also began to like him, although he would not admit it. He would however enjoy the hours of checker games they would sometimes play.

Through the years, George would occasionally see this guy. He often would visit with George when he would be home. He would always tell George that Jesus loved him. So yes, there were several folks who did try. His mom, his grandma, one of his uncles, some of the nuns, some of the preachers, some of the teachers, a fireman, and yes several different police officers had honestly tried to be of help. Their help just seemed to be too little at the moment or often it was simply much too late.

Now out in the cold again, and it was very cold this winter with warm places becoming hard to find at night. He spent his fifteenth birthday drunk on some cheap wine, out of cigarettes, and just walking around the city in the freezing cold. He slept that night under some cardboard behind some factory. He really wanted to go home, but he knew he just couldn't get along with his mom, and no one else would even trust him in their house, so the streets were his home.

By late January, he would experience some of the effects of such rejection from distrust. His older brother Marty had a wife, and by this time had three daughters, the oldest being seven years old. He had a decent job now and they had their own house, and he offered to let George come and live with them. George thought this could be great. It was still bitterly cold outside and a warm place sounded great. Besides, he missed his big brother and thought they could have some good times.

Marty had to be gone working a lot and George just sat around watching TV. After just a few days, Marty's wife did not think George was good people—which he was not! So one day, she lied to Marty and said that George had molested one of their daughters. She was only two years old. Please! George had shacked up with a thirty-year-old and a twenty-four-year-old, as well as having been with several other adults. He could be with adults. He did not need to mess with a little baby.

Well, after Marty beat the snot out of George and threw him down a flight of stairs, he told him as long as he lived to never come back. Sometime later, his wife told Marty the truth, that she just did not want George there! His brother was sorry but who cared! George did not want to stay anyway! Had George's reputation not been so, this may have been good. He needed his brother, all six feet, three inches, and 340 pounds of him!

Now in February, it was still very cold, so he goes back home for some of mom's homemade soup. He was welcomed in, as always, but the preaching started after the first day and he decides to head back west to where it was warmer. He begins hitchhiking again and catches a ride as far as St. Louis. He thinks, *Not this place again*. But catches another ride almost to Texas and then headed westward.

By April of 1974, he was somewhere in the southwest when he heard about the super outbreak of tornadoes that went through Indiana. He tries calling his mom from a payphone but lines were down. He wanted to know if she and his little brother were okay. He started drifting his way back home over the next few days. He saw a lot of damage from the storms on his way back home and was worrying more and more as he got into Indiana. It was a mess. But when he finally made it home, he was relieved and glad to see his mom was okay. She was overwhelmed with joy to see him okay, but he didn't want her crying. He told her to stop crying or he would leave. She did and for nearly a month he was home without incident. But then he just disappeared again with no heads up. He was just gone.

9

Hold the Press

One night in late April of 1974, George went back to his mom's house—stoned of course. He could barely stand. She helps him, thinking he was hurt again, but he said he wasn't. He was just too wasted to walk! He quickly passed out on the couch and she began to stew. She had been preaching to him to get a haircut and look like a man instead of a girl. His hair was down on his back again and she decided to take some clippers to it while he slept. She cut it bald on top, and hacked it up all over to make it look like a mess. She could cut hair quite well having always been a barber for the boys. The mess she made of it was to make a statement! She then called the police and told them he was there. She knew they had a warrant out for him, not paying some fines and failing to go to court.

At this point, she really had it with him. Not that she didn't love him, it was that she just couldn't take the stress anymore. He had now influenced her baby to be like him. Fred had been going out late and coming in high at all hours of the mornings, and now she was whipping him as she had George. She blamed George for this, because Fred had learned it all from him.

Well, that ended his stay with his mom that time and started a stay in jail. At the arraignment, at fifteen, Isabelle told the judge she loved George, but just could not control him and did not want him coming back around. The cops and the courts also had enough. The foster care system repeatedly failed to contain him, and he proved that he was not a mental case. The prosecuting attorney was suggesting that George be made a ward of the court and placed into a detention home until he turned eighteen.

Wait! Hold the presses! An attorney comes forward on behalf of George. He was a good drinking buddy of Otto's, and to all's surprise, in walked Otto into the courtroom and respectfully addressed the judge explaining that he had failed to be a dad and would like the chance. He would take custody and be entirely responsible for his son. He paid all his fines and court costs. This was the first time George can even recall his dad ever being sober; not only sober but also he also did not look or act like the barroom brawler George knew. Sure, his dad was sober a lot of times but somehow all he could remember was the drunk. To George's recollection, this was also the first time he would see his dad in a suit. He didn't even wear a suit to his own mother's funeral. Now, he was all cleaned up and well-groomed. And he spoke for several minutes in court without even cussing. This was clearly a different man than George knew!

Until this point, this man had, at least in part, been much of the fuel for George's rage. Otto was never around, except as a violent, disgusting drunk! For George to be rescued by someone he never felt had even expressed feelings for him and by someone he felt a passionate hatred for, only added more confusion to George's warped and demented thinking.

In the past years, since his parents separated, the only time the boys would even see their dad was on the weekends. It seemed as if he didn't want to support them unless they would come to the bars and find him. He would buy them all the sodas they could drink and, sure, occasionally George would get a few sips of this or that and occasionally would leave with a pint. Otto would let George drink all he wanted if Isabelle would have not fought him so about the booze. All the while, Isabelle felt forced into permitting the visits to the bars to get the support from him that was necessary to feed and clothe the children. But rest assured, she knew nothing about him still slipping them the booze.

Otto was their dad. He was to have visitation, and she desperately needed the money he would give her. Of course, the visits to see his dad were only until George was around ten or so, when George's bitterness now focused primarily on his dad. Everything went from being God's fault, to his mom's, to George's, to the school's, and to the legal system's failure. To finally find a resting place; now, it was entirely his dad's fault. He always had to blame someone along with himself!

George had not been around his dad much since then. Now, seeing him after all this time all cleaned up and sober was somewhat overwhelming to say the least. The last time his dad was in that court, he urinated on the courthouse steps and was arrested for threatening to kill the judge. Now a judge was going to let him take George home. George began reasoning to himself—"Could it be?" "What if?" "Well maybe!" "Perhaps he has changed!" George would not admit it, but deep down he did hope his dad had changed, and deep down he did love his dad, he just was not about to say it to the buzzard!

This was in the first part of May 1974. Now at fifteen, he was off to start a new life, living with his patriotic dear old war hero of a dad. Well, the truth is they did become pals of a sort—which was drinking buddies! His dad was so popular at all the bars. George never again had trouble being served. This was not limited to beer, but tequila, vodka, bourbon, and so on. George did get to know things about his dad that no one else knew. The war stories his mother did not want him to hear and about all the French and Italian girls and the Fräuleins. They spent that summer really catching up and getting to know each other.

One of the things he wanted George to really know was that he was a proud man, and a better man for being in that man's army. He had been celebrating the war being over now into 1974. He absolutely had every right to enjoy a time of celebrating because he had lived out part of history when the great tyrant over the world was finally removed.

But not for thirty years; not the way he was wrapped up in it. He would go on and on when he was drunk and make one of his many great toasts, "No mission is too difficult, no sacrifice too great, and duty first," and down another drink would go! This was some toast for a drunk who spoke words of respect with a forked tongue. He had deserted the mission of a dad. He would not sacrifice the booze for his children and he certainly put his current duty last!

George would begin to learn much more about his dad's childhood and life, who he really was! George would learn who had raped his dad as a boy and whom he had raped. No one else had ever known this. In telling this story, George is now betraying promises to his dad to keep this quiet. This is a promise to break! Silence of things like these causes too many destructive things. This should be a simple choice, put it on a scale, break your confidence or share in the blame for someone being broken!

His dad really was as patriotic as they come. Every morning he had a small flag hanging on a small pole mounted on the wall, and he would salute it first thing. He traditionally would say the Pledge of Allegiance. He was a baseball fan, and even when the national anthem was played over a radio, he would stand in reverence with his hand upon his heart. And if anyone was around him, and I mean anyone, who had a hat on during the anthem, they would remove it. He claimed his blood was light purple: the shade of red, white, and blue mixed. He really loved this country.

He followed all the armed forces news and events. During the Vietnam War, it was common for the vets of the past wars to nearly shun or look down on our own troops of those days, but not so with Otto. He would make patriotic toasts to the countless mentions of each fallen solder he would hear about, as if it were a close family member who had died. He would talk as if he knew something about everything military. As for the United States history, he knew the names of every president, the years they served, and the good and bad they done—according to him. He could nearly quote the Declaration of Independence, even when drunk. George was impressed as to just how smart he was. Honestly before this he had thought his dad was just a stupid old drunk.

His dad was in tight with the VFW Hall and the American Legion. Between the two of these organizations, they had access to a few actual war footage film reels that George got to see. He learned a lot about this country's history through not only the films but also his dad's friends; they were all old soldiers. For reasons unknown, his dad was about the youngest of his friends, much the same as George was younger than most of his friends. One memorable older man had fought in WWI; several had fought in WWII, and some in the Korean War.

George had the privilege to hear firsthand stories from those who lived through the battles. He heard stories from those who had served in virtually every branch of the armed forces. At the American Legion, they had a TV going most of the time; and the guys there were always up to date on everything in the news, and generally were all skeptics of what was going on. This skepticism went completely through the Vietnam War, the Cuban missile crisis and Watergate. Some of the hottest current topics of discussion were about India now becoming the sixth power having the bomb and about the Watergate scandal and President Nixon.

For quite some time around his dad and his friends, drugs of any kind weren't used. He was too fascinated by the captivating war stories to even want to hang out with his friends during this time. Besides, he had all the beer he could ever ask for. He would also have some privileged access to some after hours closed events at a couple of bars. He was, more often than not, in a half-drunken state at home.

As for school, in mid-August he was sent to a special school for troubled children. This school and its teachers were an absolute joke. George smoothly slid through there. You see, he had a history of being a drug supplier for one of the teachers. Some may find it hard to believe that a school teacher could be controlled by a student, but George was not your ordinary fifteen-year-old. His time at this vocational school was not long, only about three or four months and he was put back into the public system. By this time, he was nearing sixteen and was relocated and placed—or should I say—dropped into the ninth grade.

He, in all honesty, could not read more than see spot run! Unlike before, these new kids did not know he was tough or cool; he was faced with proving it all again. He was getting tired of all the fighting, as well as afraid of all the new changes. Yes, afraid. He had many untold fears that only went unnoticed.

Besides, there was really little for him at this school, except someone to sell drugs or stolen goods to. That is unless it was a couple of the girls he hit it off with. Besides, he could get the girls and make money without school. When he turned sixteen, the court would not touch him for quitting! He knew he had to just play it cool and stick it out for a couple months, so he did. George was then going to be off to face life with possibly little more than a second- to third-grade level. The educational system failed him, as it has countless thousands of others.

It was finally George's sixteenth birthday and George was tired of it all. Life had to have more to offer than the shady hand he was dealt! So running was on his mind again! Perhaps fantasizing that life could be better somewhere else. As for dear old dad, well he knew the fun would have to end. Besides, George just could not get past the anger he felt toward his dad. He was just a disappointment to his dad anyway, because one thing was clear: George was strictly not army material. He absolutely would not submit to authority of any kind.

He began to think of how to tell his dad he quit school and to say bye to his dear old dad. Finally, George wanted to go partying with his dad. That's when George thought he would tell him. However, Otto had prior plans with his army buddies, and for some reason, didn't want to hang out with George, but he did not just leave George at home alone. He left him with his birthday present, a fifth of Seagram's Seven whiskey, which surely George would be glad to drink!

George, as many drunks do, began to have pity on himself. Then to make it worse he popped a few pills. By the time Otto got home sometime into the morning hours, the whiskey and the black beauties had done their work. George came from nowhere with a nightstick and busted his dad wide open, knocking him to the floor. He just sat there looking at George and began to cry. Yes, cry. This mighty war hero who had fought so bravely in the military and this Leroy Brown type of barroom brawler, who was thought to be an ice cube—the pure example of cold and tough—was crying like a baby.

Puzzled by knowing that his dad could have whipped him, but he instead just cried as a little child. George would always remember those tears as they mixed with the gushing blood. He repeatedly and very earnestly asked George, "Why, why, why? How could you hit your dad?" George wanted him to fight and began kicking him repeatedly but he would just not hit back. He just cried. Amazingly, George photographically embossed a memory of his face being entirely bloody while still recalling the distinction of the tears. He also would never forget that this incident was the first time he spoke the words that George could never imagine hearing from his dad. He asks, "Don't you know I love you?"

Perhaps in utter shock, George just hit him again and stepped over his bloody body as if he was just a pile of trash. George just left, not knowing or caring if his dad would live or die. He had beaten him badly, took all his money, and left! He later discovered that his dad had four broken ribs, a dislocated shoulder, a broken jaw, a broken nose, and required several stitches. His dad told the police that he had been mugged and could not identify the assaulter. George did not see or contact his dad for around the next five years. George was sure his dad remembered it was him, but perhaps he was just too drunk to even remember.

Over the next few months, George just drifted around the area. The hookers cared for him if he had drugs or money. He would mug someone for a few bucks here and there. He robbed houses and train cars, shoplifted from grocery stores, and sold any dope he and his hooker friends did not use! George occasionally spent a night in jail for disorderly conduct. That was just a twenty-five-dollar fine and his little brother would bring it up and they would let him out.

The cops knew these two boys but still had never had any problems with his little brother. They knew he was not able to get along with his mom and that his dad was as he was, they knew! What were they to do with George? They honestly felt that he just didn't have them all. A few different times during this winter, on the coldest nights, just to keep warm he would do something petty to be busted over. After all, it was three hots and a cot in a warm room. Once, when it was freezing cold outside, he walked into the police station and mooned the dispatcher.

This stuff just never justified the right judge in sending a sixteen-year-old to an overpopulated and underfunded juvenile center, but it would get him a night or two out of the cold weather, and perhaps a trip to the stress center for a few weeks. They told him several times that they were letting him go because sooner or later they were going to get something better on him and he would be going down for a long time.

However, George always evaded anyone from actually getting the goods on him. Several times he had been pulled in for questioning by detectives about this job or that one. His involvement in several bigger heists was implied, but never proven. Now he starts drifting from one big city to another, drifting through the smaller towns, and with the help of his older acquaintances, his spree occasionally then went across several states.

Although George seems to find a place to stay from one night to the next or from one week to the next week, technically, he was homeless with no means of stability, void of any type of structure or routine. This purely spontaneous life was full of the fear of the unknown; he called it an adventure!

The larger cities were the most attractive to him, but he often seemed to get caught up in some kind of trouble in between them. He had just got into Detroit to meet up with a biker friend who he had sold drugs for. One of his newer lady friends went with him to meet this dude. This guy told him they could turn some fast cash if they could drop a package in Denver but the girl would have to stay behind, so off they went in a pickup truck. Just after dark they got into some little town in Illinois just across the river from St. Louis of all places. They stopped at a strip joint to get some food and a couple of drinks. Unlike some of the bars George had gotten into, this one would not let him in. His friend said he would bring him something out, so he stayed in the truck.

George was already wasted and ended up passed out in the truck. Some unknown time later he was awakened by his friend beating on the door. There was blood all over; he was cut up really badly with a machete, and he told George he thought he killed a guy. George got him in the truck and started driving. He thought his friend was dying; his forearm seemed like it was barely hanging on and some of his stomach innards were exposed. George was not straight enough to drive so he stopped the truck in a different neighborhood and got his friend to the porch of a house. He told George to leave him and just make the delivery.

George beat on the door a couple times and made for the truck. He never knew about that guy again. He put the truck in a ditch just a few miles from there; grabbed the dope, it was in a duffel bag; and he hitched a ride with a trucker to Oklahoma City.

As for the stuff that was supposed to go to Denver, it didn't quite make it. He first sells some of the drugs to get a bus ticket to Denver, but while he waits on the bus to arrive, he meets a girl in the terminal who was headed to Wichita, Kansas. The next thing you know he changes plans to head to Denver after he goes to Wichita. Once there she took him to her place not far from the bus station. Unfortunately for George, right in the middle of the deed, five or six of her friends came in, beat him up, and took everything he had.

He woke up the next day next to a big trash dumpster buck naked with no memory, and a cop was shaking him.

They took him to a hospital and he played stupid, as if he did not even know who he was or what had happened. He overheard them say they were going to transfer him to a mental hospital. He had been in more than one of these and knew it was as hard to get out of there as it was to escape jail. So he swiped some clothes from a closet across the hall from his room, and he was gone.

He spent that night in pain in a large drainage ditch to get somewhat out of the rainstorm, but it was so noisy from the rushing water going through that he could not sleep much. It was beginning to get light the next morning and the rain stopped. He just laid there and went to sleep. To his surprise it was dark when he woke up. He struggled to get moving. He was pretty beaten up. He started down the road not even knowing where he was. He aimlessly walked for what seemed to be hours, then nearing exhaustion and just after daylight, he finds another ditch and rests for a bit. But when he woke up, it was evening, and he began walking again. He gets into a smaller town just before it was dark, and he sees some guy sitting on a porch and asks him what town it was and if he had a smoke. He told George that this is Maize, Kansas, and George collapsed.

The man leads George into their house and tells him he will call for help, and George quickly tells him no. The man says, "I see, okay!" The man said, "At least let my wife fix you a good supper and get you out of these clothes." The clothes he had taken from the hospital didn't fit. The shirt was too small and it had torn and the pants were too long, and he was barefooted and still half wet. The woman said they had a son who had moved out who was about his size. They imposed kindness and he needed some of that. He took a hot bath, got into a clean set of clothes, and had an excellent meal. The lady insisted on doing a bit of doctoring to George's eye and lip, and it kind of reminds him of his mom.

The man asks where he was from, and George told him Indianapolis and told him he was trying to get back to see his mom and got robbed. They let George use the phone to call his mom—who else could he call? The man told George that he would drive him to the bus station in the morning and pay for his fare home. "Meanwhile, you need some rest," the woman said that she had made a bed for him. At the moment George thought to himself they were nuts and or they were going to call the cops on him after he fell asleep, so his thinking was to just pretend to be asleep and sneak out. But he was dead tired and fell fast asleep anyway.

The next morning, the man knocked on the door and told George that breakfast was ready. He was in disbelief that they didn't call the cops. After breakfast, as he was leaving with the man to go to the bus station, the lady gently grabbed him by the arm pulling him close and softly said she would be praying for him. That was that; that never added nothing but a smile and gave George twenty dollars in a handshake when he said, "So long," at the bus station.

As George was now on his way back home, he thought that it would have been cool to have had parents like them. It dawned on him that the night before, when he went into the bedroom to dress, he had stolen a wallet that was laying on a shelf and it had twenty dollars in it, and he briefly felt sorry. Then he looked into the wallet, and instead of finding the money, it had a handwritten letter in it that George wasn't able to read. When he got home, he shows the letter to his mom. The letter read:

> This was my son's wallet, he died in Vietnam and the twenty dollars I handed you was his too. Son, just always know that someone is praying for you!

"That stupid old goat," George said. His mom said, "No, he wasn't stupid. He was just doing what God wanted him to do." She insisted that God had been protecting him. He grumbled at this with sarcasm, saying; "God never protected me, never has, don't give me that xxxx, I wouldn't be beat up now if He protected me."

He stayed at home this time for about two weeks. He was really hurt. He had about six broken ribs and lost a couple teeth in that last mess. Besides, his mom was some cook and was quite experienced at nursing the boys back to health. The truth was he had really missed his mom; he gives her a kiss and tells her he loves her. She begins to cry and George starts cussing and telling her if she can't keep her mouth shut with the crying he was just leaving again. She calms down and he stays a few more days.

But the word was out that he was back, and there were some bikers asking about him and he knew what that meant. He was supposed to drop five pounds of weed and a mess of pills off to a biker's house in Denver. The dope was all gone and he better be gone too.

Once he had spent a few days in a county jail with one of his older brother's friends, his name was Mark. He lived near Nashville, Tennessee. He had come through once in a while and stopped by the house, and once told George if he ever needed a place to go to call him. His mom gets the number for him, and George gives him a call and he said, "Come on down." He had halfway confessed to his mom and told her these biker guys were going to kill him if they caught him, and he just wasn't healed enough to take off hitchhiking. So she gave him some cash for another bus ticket.

He got to Nashville, and Mark met him at the bus station. He hung out there for about a month and had been getting pretty close to the guy's younger sister. She was heavy into bestiality and a bunch of weird stuff even to George. But he didn't seem to mind; it was through this relationship he also partook on some new experiences. He recalls her as the girl most likely to drink a fifth of Jack Daniel's and walk a straight line. She could handle more booze than perhaps even his dad could have.

She was about twenty and going to move to Memphis with another one of her brothers. She said it was cool for George to come too, so he did. The house was some distance outside of Memphis out in the country; it was up some really steep hills.

George was a party guy and had been around the dope scene a whole lot. There was little he hadn't seen, so he thought. Her brother's house was huge and George was at awe when he went inside. The reefer smoke was so thick you could get stoned in the entry without taking a toke. As you walked toward the living room, you went through a series of beads hanging in the doorways; there was black velvet and fluorescent-colored wallpaper all over. It had what was seemingly hundreds of candles lighting the house. In the living room, there was a strobe light in each corner hanging above each of four of the best-sounding speakers money could buy, powered by a state-of-the-art quad amp.

The floor was shaking from the base and in the center of the ceiling was the biggest disco ball glittering with the reflections from the strobes and several black lights filling the area. Then he saw it, the largest octopus he had ever seen. This guy had bongs and pipes of every sort lying around, but this octopus was something extra special. It had to be about four feet tall and had eight long hoses. It was surrounded by a round couch. This thing was custom-made for this guy, and it must have held close to a half pound. The drugs were of every sort and in abundant amounts. Acid was the house specialty but during this time, George liked the weed and the booze more than the cocaine or LSD. This would be home for the next two or three months, and he thought it was the greatest place he had ever stayed; it was like a party boy's heaven.

While he is hanging out there, he learns that this house wasn't actually her brother's, it was a cop's. He was the one who brought them the dope. It was said that this and other cops would stop someone with dope and instead of arresting them he would just take the dope. George's girlfriend then tells him this cop was one of the main suppliers for the area. George, like most wannabe-hoodlums, thought this was the coolest thing ever, to have a free ticket to party without the threat of the cops.

One evening George rode with one of the guys into town to help pick up some grub. The next thing you know, George was coming out of a store, and the cops grabbed him, shoved him in a car, and in minutes, were pumping him for information. The detectives asked a bunch of questions about the house and about the man who lived there, and questioned if he had seen any police at the house. George played stupid and told them he was just hiking through town. They ran his prints, checked for warrants, and he came up clean for a change, so after they held him a couple days they let him go and told him to hike on, so he hit the road again.

He would have no recollection of this Christmas passing him by, he would not even recall seeing any Christmas decorations that year. By seventeen, George's adventure curiosity would have taken him to several states west of the Mississippi, as well as to some eastern ones, and from north to south. Whether by train, by thumb or on a bus, alone or with a girl, or with just another doper, he would just go. This often would lead him to cold or hot places. He recalled often being hungry. On several occasions, he was either beaten up or beat someone up to get food along the way. Perhaps this was his fantasy search for a happy place, away from his disturbed childhood!

He wasn't really always so wasted he lost track of times, like Christmas, New Years, and even his birthday as he had just done. He would recall many days that he had no drugs or booze, and many weeks at a time with no memory lapses. He was nowhere near the stone-cold hoodlum or thug as he would have some to believe, but he wasn't as innocent as he would have others believing either. He was a mixture of characters in one, with the ability to adapt as a chameleon and would simply blend in. This was nothing like having random or triggered multiple personalities; this was strategic, and it was at will. It was a well-developed craft. It seemed to George as if the police couldn't get a substantial charge against him. He just always appeared to be a step ahead or just plain lucky.

It was as if he took pride in how well he could lie, and no doubt he was excellent at it. Crime labs of that day also had not progressed to the capabilities of using DNA; the forensics of this time was yet somewhat in the dinosaur age. Also technology had not advanced to have metal detectors and video surveillance everywhere, and GPS tracking was only found in science-fiction movies. The bottom line was that it appeared he could do anything and just get out of it. Whether it was from poor police work or from his ability to lie, it just really didn't matter as long as he was free.

At just a couple months over seventeen, in March of 1976, the fun things in life had already drawn him so far into the darkness that light was no longer visible, as his mother would say. The law of averages would however finally catch up to him. He had told one of his friends about all the guns his uncle had. His friend had a car so they drove down to see his uncle but his uncle wasn't home. George knew where a key was kept outside, so they went on in. This uncle was the one George thought the most of. He was always treated great by him, and George always behaved for him. But now George and his friend stole as many of the working guns and ammunition as they could pack into the trunk and away they went. They then sold all the stuff except one gun; the .30-06 that was his and his mom's favorite gun.

He then brought that gun back to his mom's and hid it in her basement. What was he thinking? Of all the places to leave it, he had stashed it at his Bible-thumping mother's. She found it, naturally recognizing it as her brother's. She had already heard that her brother had been robbed. She immediately turned it into the police and told them where George was staying. She was thinking that if he didn't kill someone and end up going away for life, they were going to find him dead somewhere. They thought perhaps he still had some of the weapons. They hit the house where he was staying with what appeared to be twenty cops and the state police.

They knew he had help. He had no car and over fifty guns had been stolen. The police knew he could lead them to the rest of the guns or tell them what happened to them. But he knew they only had the goods on him, and he wasn't talking. He figured he was a juvenile and if it comes to it, he could play the mental card. He felt confident he would walk out of this mess also, but the police wanted those guns. They knew it was his friend, who he was staying with, who was part of it, but they had no evidence on him so he was never charged.

Isabelle came to see him in the county jail. She then told George, "You made your bed, you sleep in it!" She thought that she had done her best, now the state could have a crack at trying to train him. She told him she had talked to his uncle, and he said to tell him he forgives him, that when he gets out to come see him and he would tell him what the thing was that he was so afraid of. George had bugged him to tell him that for a few years. George just tells his mom he was mad at her and not to come back anymore. He was done with her forever. He hated her for what she had done.

She would never uphold anyone in wrongdoing. At the same time, she would defend a stranger to death if the stranger was right. This was her way since he could remember. When he was four, when he would steal gum or candy, she would make him take it back to the store and confess to what he had done. Once when he was five, she even threatened to beat up a store owner. When George told him he had stolen some candy, the owner said, "That's okay!" Not with Isabelle, it was not! No one was going to tell her son that was okay! The store owner was behind the meat counter during this and quickly apologized to Isabelle and took George behind the counter where he had been grinding meet and told George if he ever stole anything in his store again he would make hamburger out of him. This of course never deterred George, but it adds depth about his mom's character.

George spent the next week sitting in the local county jail. Here, he was really in need of some medical assistance to address the DTs. This wasn't a new experience for him. He had suffered withdrawal on several past occasions. But in a mental ward of a hospital they give you enough other drugs that you don't crash quite so hard. But jail was no hospital. About the second day he was jailed it started. By the morning of the third day, the cold sweats, high fever, pounding heartbeats, and the shivering shakes had overwhelmed him. He was under such distress and high anxiety he remembered little more about this week.

Then he was extradited from Indiana to Missouri to a small county jail in the country. In his first few days here the anxiety from withdrawal slowly faded but his cravings continued. He would then sit there for nearly seven months awaiting trial. He was now facing his first adult felony conviction before he was eighteen. He had been appointed a public defender, and he told George there was nothing he could do to help him. He assured George he was going down for this.

There were a few notable things about this jail and his stay there. George was treated with respect. He was not beaten or even pushed around by anyone. The officers always acted friendly, unlike most he had known. For the most part, there were but just a few inmates. It was rather a small jail. There was a fella who would bring the food and it was like his mom's. The only thing that seemed to be missing was Barney Fife. It comes with great food and a friendly atmosphere. There was even a regular who would come in drunk every Saturday evening. They had a drunk tank, and this fella would wobble straight for it, and the way he talked you would think he felt like it was his very own personal room.

This man would sing Gospel songs often till very early Sunday mornings. He was really a mental case. George knew he himself wasn't all together upstairs, but this guy was really wacko. He would try telling the other inmates they were going to hell if they didn't become Christians. But when someone would make a wisecrack or remark, he would begin cussing them out, telling them he was the one who was going to throw them into a lake of fire. He really was messed up.

But boy this man could really sing, as if he was a star or somebody special.

George asked one of the deputies what was wrong with him. He said that man used to be a minister at a small church, but one Saturday evening after a singing at the church, he chose to stay and pray. His wife and three small children were on their way home and were killed in a car accident by a drunk driver. The grief sent him into such a state of depression that he was replaced by another minister, and then he started drinking and was pretty much abandoned by church people and he just kept getting worse. But like clockwork, he was singing his songs every Saturday evening. From then on, George never teased him. He wouldn't listen to his preaching, but he wouldn't make fun of him either and would start yelling at anyone else that made fun of him.

In the later part of George's stay there, about the week before his court date, a man is placed into the cell next to him. He was facing a murder charge and was a Bible thumper. He was a deacon of a local church. He had a teenage daughter who had a boy chasing after her and he kept coming to their house. He said he had kept telling him to stay away. But one night he found that he had snuck in through a window. The man claimed, as he ran off, he intended to just fire over his head, but shot him in the head instead, killing him.

This man started talking to George. He really had nothing better to do. The deputy would frequently let George go into his cell so they could play checkers. As they talked, for some unknown reason, George kind of opens up to this man. As a summary, the man tells George it sounds a lot like you have burnt all your bridges. He tells George that if you ever want another bridge to try, ask God. Although the God thing meant nothing to George, the thought that he really had burnt all his bridges would stick with him for some time. He didn't really try preaching at George, or he wouldn't have got the time of day from him. He was just a normal guy who was in jail, just like George.

Then a box of cookies came from his mom. He shared them with the deacon in the next cell. It would appear all his friends had abandoned him; no visitors, no mail, no calls. George had plenty so he shared. Then like clockwork, the jail's favorite drunk came wobbling in, singing his songs of peace, love, and joy. George had some cookies passed to him also. He says, "Maybe they would shut him up." But deep down inside, he knew that he had been experiencing a peaceful time in this jail.

10

Game Changer

Now with just over six months before he was to turn eighteen, with the evidence his mother had turned in, he was headed up to see the judge for sentencing. His lawyer told him, if it wasn't that the weapons were stolen and if he had already turned eighteen before the burglary, he may have been able to get more leniency, because they likely would not have used his whole juvenile record against him. In addition, if he would just cooperate and tell the police what happened to the guns, but he would not. But as it was, the judge would not go there and neither would a jury. Taking stolen guns across state lines broke more than just state law; the FBI also wanted to know about the rest of the guns and George just remained quiet.

His lawyer explained this was not going away this time, he was! If it went to trial, he was told he would likely be looking at fifteen to twenty years. If he plea-bargained out, he would only get five. By this time back home, they had several other drug charges awaiting his release and were willing to drop them if he would take this five. He discussed leaning on mental problems for leniency. His lawyer then explained they would place him in a state mental hospital until he was able to face the charges; these charges were not just going away. They wanted to know where the rest of the guns went and who helped him. The judge gave him another chance; he said a cuss word to the judge and he still wouldn't tell, so the hammer fell.

He was sentenced to spend the next five years in the Missouri State Penitentiary. His lawyer told him he could be out on parole in about another eighteen months if he kept his nose clean. He would however be able to use his jail time toward his time. In just a couple days, he was shipped out to his new home. This would be in a prison where he was unknown. George had friends incarcerated in Indiana, Illinois, and Tennessee, but none that were in Missouri. This seemed to be more of a concern to him, than the joint (prison) itself.

The Department of Corrections is perhaps the most underrated type of school or college. The sick and demented criminal elements within George's mind were vastly enhanced through imprisonment. What and from whom he would learn from in this place, would prepare him to leave capable of being a more dangerous thug! Inmates convicted of less violent crimes and those with shorter sentences were intended to be placed into minimum- to medium-security facilities. Some even to farm-like places, some with doors in place of bars. However, actual placement was based on availability. The system was so overpopulated at that time especially the farm-type facilities, as a result he was sent behind the walls, into the historic maximum-security prison, with the "big boys"!

This place was known as the Walls. Just a few years earlier, *Time* magazine had called it the bloodiest forty-seven acres in America. It not only was a dangerous place with some really bad people but also it was also the oldest continually operating prison west of the Mississippi. At one time, it was the largest prison in the United States.

George initially entered prison with some mixed and false ideas about what to expect. He had known many who were sent up and was aware of homosexuals and the street savvy needed to overcome. Perhaps due to some hidden guilt about his experiments with his younger brother, he was quite homophobic. He would die before engaging in this.

He had some idea that prison might just be like going to a new school, where all he would have to do was to prove he was tough or cool. Thinking that you could just pick out the biggest meanest-looking one, kick him in the shins, and gain respect! Well, he was about to learn something; the things others had told him was 75 percent bologna, 15 percent cheese, and 10 percent crackers.

He was quickly shown, that it was not that simple, as well as clearly learning that he was not as tough as he thought. He proved to be little more than an uneducated, smart-mouthed, punk kid, with the wannabe-Bruce Lee attitude! In this house, there were plenty of real tough guys capable of making him realize this.

He did however show persistency with his efforts. He was determined to fit in. However, finding a way for a seventeen-year-old to adapt to this environment quickly proved this was not going to be easy. Unlike on the streets where his karate style of street fighting had him winning nineteen out of twenty fights; that 90 percent of the time he picked. Here, he was only one in twenty, and he didn't need to pick or necessarily get to pick too many of these fights. This was not too good for such a real bad dude! He did have enough heart and street-smarts that eventually gained some respect, or at least took some of the focus off him. But to say that his smart mouth had been wiped off was an understatement. He was certainly made to realize he had to stop his random mouthing off.

He quickly stopped looking for the fight, but would never back out of fighting. He would not conform to system rules, yet respected the unwritten inmate rules. He knew how to keep his eyes and ears open for himself, while never seeing or hearing anything! Naturally, he knew how to keep his mouth shut! This was essential toward saving not only his manhood but also his neck!

Your average man wants sex, and when they are locked up and can't get any, an array of things will happen, especially within the confined and among the demented. Some will just want, some will masturbate, others will seek pleasure in activities with—or from—others! Most will give their right arm for a page out of a pornographic magazine. However, only a very extremely few just sit idly by and want! George wanted to just be another typical man and leaned toward the porn. Pornographic materials were considered contraband; however, it seemed to not only make it inside but also it was tolerated to an extent by the screws (guards).

The belief that men are raped in prison has a lot of credibility—it really does happen. However, there are usually some contributing factors that go with the majority of rape cases. The highest risks are to those who are incarcerated for rape or molestation charges. Or if you are already gay or display a feminine-like attitude. Others at risk are those labeled as a snitch. In many sexual abuse cases, the end result commonly depends on the individual. For example, if you are such a wimp that you're not willing to fight to keep your manhood, someone will surely try to scare you into giving it up! This was not to say that rape didn't happen outside these factors, it was just that most were from like circumstances.

Finally, playing cards would prove to be one of the helpful methods of survival, He was very good and could win a valuable commodity—cigarettes! At this time, not only was smoking allowed in prison but also the state would also give tobacco to inmates. Not too many actually liked the issued pouches of Bull Durham tobacco or to even roll their own. They traded things from the commissary, the mess hall, or from the yard, for tailor-made smokes! A single cigarette could often be traded for someone's dessert. A pack could be traded for the last month's centerfold and two packs would get you this month's edition. A carton could purchase a shank; five cartons could get someone *shanked!*

It didn't take him long to figure out how to tap into the supply line. With this came new acquaintances and the type of popularity that protected him to an extent. In fact, when he won, it would seem blending in with the hardened criminals was easier than functioning in society ever was. The problem was that no one always wins, and when he had no smokes he lost his friends.

In this time era, when an inmate is put into population, they are assigned a job. George felt lucky that he was assigned kitchen duty. This meant that George would eat when the kitchen workers ate. Not with the general population. George was on the floor crew. His job was cleaning and mopping the kitchen floor. Working here had some notable benefits. If someone were an enemy of a kitchen worker, their food might have human waste in it, or worse. The homosexuals and snitches and those in check in or protective custody would often have something extra in their food. The kitchen workers were not as likely to have such in their food. George saw many such sick things, yet, at the time, he thought they were funny. George would go on to instigate all sorts of sick and demented things. He didn't care if other inmates had to eat it. Seemingly forgetting that the forty-five days prior to getting assigned to the kitchen, he had eaten what was cooked from the kitchen himself.

As he watched time go by, he sees his Christmas pass, then his eighteenth birthday. Although he received no visitors, he would frequently get letters from his mom telling him about what all was happening back home. He would have his cellmate help him read them when he could not. By this time, his little brother Fred, whom his mom thought would never do anything wrong, was convicted of armed robbery. This was before he had even turned sixteen. He was sent to detention and was to remain there until he turned eighteen. She would also tell George about everything else that went on back home. About who else had gotten sick, or came down with this disease, or that one. About her best friend, who had died, as well as this one or that one getting arrested, dying, or getting killed.

One day, she sent George a letter telling him his uncle John, who he spent the summers with and who he stole the guns from, had passed away. He became enraged and beat his fist hitting the wall of his cell until he had no energy left. He loved this uncle, but never told him. He had written George a letter and told him that when he gets out, if he would come to see him he would tell George what he was afraid of. This was the big question that George had for years now. He had been trying to get him to tell and now he would never know.

Now with his hands all bloody and swollen up, a guard noticed and insisted taking him to see the doctor. Then because he wouldn't say what happened, he was sent to the hole for ten days, thinking he had been in a fight. While there, he quickly began thinking he wasn't going to be able to hold cards as well for a few days, and knew he certainly wasn't going to be in shape to do too much fighting for a while. He understood he needed to find another edge, or he was going to be in for some hard times. But what?

While he was in the hole, out on the block, his cellmate was hurt really bad in a fight and had went into check-in. When he got out of the hole, he now had a new cellmate. This guy was some burnout from the sixties and was in his upper forties. He had previously spent a dime (ten years), and was said to have only been out on parole for a month before he was busted again. Now he was starting twenty-five more years in addition to finishing his first sentence. This guy not only knew the ropes but also was willing to show them to George. He must have had a son or a kid brother about George's age. Friends were only superficial in prison, but these two acted more like real brothers.

He teaches George a new game. As new inmates came in, they were going to be first placed in a cell on H-hall while processed through. As part of the process, all dignity is left outside: you are strip-searched, deloused, and introduced to the doctor known as Old Gold Finger! It would seem everyone would watch them come down the walk, like whistling at beautiful women. The funny thing was that this had happened when each and every one of them came through. It was kind of like a welcome party or an initiation. The cons seemed to know all about them before they ever made it to population. How much time you had and what it was for. George and his cellmate would take cigarette bets with other inmates on which ones would put their soap on a rope or be the first one they would hear crying for mommy in the night and so on. He won a lot at this, while other cons were watching them to see who was scared. George knew they were all scared, just as he was.

He seemed to effortlessly sort the submissive from the controlling personalities. This made George valuable to various types of aggressors. This type of profiling was practiced and taught in the prison systems long before police officers on the streets were trained in profiling! George received a master's degree in this field in just a short while. He very successfully predicted the submissive, letting them know who to best target, while he accumulated the cigarettes for the bets!

Once, George was watching the walk and realized what a small world this was. From states away, he recognized someone from the past. They had bad blood between them, because George had slept with his wife and this guy beat the tar out of George. However, the other inmates didn't know that! George then fingered him as the one who snitched on him and got him sent to the joint! He never told no one his mom had actually ratted him out, he had always claimed some other dude snitched on him.

This guy was not a snitch and had nothing to do with his situation, George just didn't like him. Some inmates that were George's frequent cigarette customers, or the predators that he fed leads to, took turns with him. They had raped and beat him until at last he broke. Within just a few weeks, he was said to walk and talk like a woman and was working for cigarettes, like a hooker on a street corner. It would appear hollering "snitch" in prison was much like hollering "fire" in a crowded theater.

Originally what George had in mind was the kitchen treatment. He thought they would do something to his food or maybe beat him up, but he really didn't expect this. It never crossed his mind they would go that far. However, after they did, George just laughed knowing what he had caused, thinking he was so smart. He had learned the art of manipulation too well and was enjoying what he thought were the benefits of being so smart. George had seen how cigarettes paid for a lot of horrific things to be done to some inmates. Having them was having power or targeted you for a thief.

This was a prison and there were really no actual thieves here, honestly just innocent victims of society. You could ask anyone there, they were all innocent. Not! Another factor was that there were limits on how many cigarettes you were allowed to purchase from the commissary, and with time on your hands, most smoked more than they were permitted to buy. Those who didn't smoke also become valuable because they could get their share for you.

George's cellmate offered basic protection for some of the scared younger inmates for two cartons a month. Then he would give a carton a month to someone to act as if they were somewhat watching out for them. A couple guys would stage a fight with the guy, then the defender would interrupt, giving the illusion that he was protecting the guy. As a result, the victim was glad to hand over more smokes. If he got wise to it or begin to feel he didn't need protection, an extra carton could be invested to let him know he needed it.

Another factor was shuffling the cigarettes. There were limits on the number of cartons you could possess in your cell. A shake down could lose you some smokes, and perhaps even get you some time in the hole. This generated the need for a constant flow, not a stockpile. If the surplus exceeded a few cartons, others who didn't smoke was employed to hold the smokes for you. Also if you was holding a large amount of anything, you became targeted for theft. This at times proved it could be quite a complex racket, which demanded careful planning.

Can the Department of Corrections in itself actually reform anyone? Not likely! The guards always seemed too occupied just corralling the inmates like cattle and trying to just prevent them from harming others, to actually do any reforming. Through the frequent and random shakedowns, anyone could still get pretty much anything for a price. It was said that for a price some guards would bring some things inside.

George himself had little trouble getting pills, or hooch, which is homemade wine, but weed was a different story. It was occasionally smelt once every week or so, but he personally only got one toke throughout this time. His skills with the cards and on the walk gained him the types of friends whom you would certainly not want to go play in this "yard" with. The typical way was you had to fend for yourself to save face. There was usually no one watching your back unless you were paying for it. This was usually reserved for the very wealthy or those with powerful friends. After just months in there, if George had a problem with someone, he didn't necessarily need to take care of it. Without asking, someone else often took care of it for him! But then it was as if you owed them something in return. This still wouldn't mean you didn't constantly need to be ready to defend yourself. This was an intense place and your guard could never be down— not for a minute or you would suffer some sort of ordeal.

By the time he had been there nine or ten months, George had adapted too well. His impulsive behavior mixed with his savvy to mind his own affairs had made him feel at home. Many lifers or those with very long sentences were the only ones that actually drank the poison of becoming institutionalized, but George was sample tasting a bit of it by beginning to feel at home. He thought this must have been kind of like his dad had must have felt. Even after WWII was over he volunteered to stay in Europe.

As the time passes by, the only thing that prison would prove to constructively accomplish for George was through the few different times he was put into the hole. The "hole" is solitary confinement. Fighting would usually come with a mandatory ten days minimum in the hole, regardless of who started it. If a guard saw some guy walk up and take a swing at you, even if he didn't actually hit you, you both would go to the hole unless you were willing to write a statement against the other guy (which was snitching). Other violations may carry longer stays. Some did nothing with the time in the hole. This gave George time alone to process all that had taken place in his life.

His last trip to the hole before his release was for nearly three months. He had been in the shower area one day and a fight had taken place. Someone was shanked (stabbed). They put everyone in the hole that was in that area, five in all. The question was, "Who shanked the guy?" Three others told the guards they didn't see who did it, but George ran away from the shower stalls telling the others something was going down and to clear out. This only left one other who could have done it. Two of the men named the one who did it, but they said they didn't actually see it done, but they had seen the other man come out of the shower with a bloody towel. The guards knew George saw what happened, but he would not say.

They kept telling him they would place him in protective custody if he would tell them who did it. He laughed at them knowing the truth of what would happen should he talk. As a result of his stubbornness, they just kept him in the hole, one of the guards had heard a distant yell, that George was next if he talked. One guard told him he was being kept there for his own good, another told him he needed to just tell who did it. The guards tried playing games like the inmates did but wasn't nearly as good at it. So in the hole he stayed. In here, the only personal item you could have was a Bible. You only left this concrete-and-steel closet of a room for the occaisional shower or on Sunday to go to the chapel. Besides that, this room was a dining room, rec room, bedroom, and bathroom; all in one.

Some thirty plus days after he was in the hole, he was pulled out to go before the parole board. He never thought he had a chance of making it and was planning on smarting off to them. But the first thing they did was tell him that due to overpopulation he would be paroled within the next thirty to forty-five days. Wow, he never saw that coming! Considering he had been in the hole three times before this time, he never gave parole a thought.

With only a little over a month to go, he began to ask himself, "What then?" He just knew that he would end up like many of the guys inside. He would be back! He recognized the similarities in their lives. He didn't want to come back, but neither did the three and four timers. And on the outside, he knew the booze and drugs would not only call to him but also they would be easily available.

He concluded that something had to change and he knew it would not be the city. He would have some paper to walk, which is parole. Should he just start running again when he got out, whenever they caught him, he would have to come back and finish the five years. He asked himself, knowing he would not make it unless he changed. If he could change, how? The thought of freedom scared him, if that makes any sense. Inside, everyone seemed to hear dark voices. He was as they were. However, outside he would be alone with only the voices! He knew he was guilty of so many bad things that no one could ever forgive, let alone forget. Dark things that he would never speak of. However, he then remembered something his mother taught him. That was, "Jesus could and would forgive and forget all sins!"

He had been so angry with God for so long for allowing this all to happen to him that he fought against letting God in. He was truly alone and no one cared. Could this turmoil be all that life had for him? If so, he no longer wanted to live. George began thinking perhaps he was at his final crossroad. There was nowhere to hide from the voices. Nothing had ever worked. There was no place to run that he had not already ran. He began to wonder if suicide was the only solution left?

He was amazed that he had even lived as long as he had. George's mind was in shambles; a total state of despair. If he could not make it on the outside, he didn't want to live. He knew he needed to cross a bridge of change. Regardless, there was no one who would help him. Any and all bridges he had in the past were burned long ago. And he remembered that guy who told him about God's bridge, but that was the very one he did not want to cross. Yes, the only bridge left was Christ! Not a chance! George knew he was unsalvageable. He was damaged goods and he knew it! He should consider that bridge burned also.

The next Sunday morning, to get some time out of the hole, George went to the chapel thinking of those bridges. Guess what the chaplain spoke on—bridges! As if he had read George's mind, that was something no head shrink could ever do! The chaplain didn't just hit and miss, he hit nails right on the head. George watched his life unfold in the chaplain's words. His life came and went before him, and as it was all destroyed, he saw the desertlike wasteland consuming everything around him, leaving only one bridge before him.

The chaplain gave an altar call, as he always had. Seldom, if any, ever go up for prayer, except the wimps who were crying for mommy. George knew he had to go, and without hesitation, he went straight down and knelt in front of the other giggling inmates and he crossed that bridge! After the chaplain had prayed with him, leading him in the sinner's prayer, and after years and years of no tears, he was crying and the tears were flowing. Then when George rose up, he noticed that another prisoner had gone down for prayer. The inmate approached George. It was the one who he had seen stab the other guy. He asks George, "Why are you crying?" George looked at him and asked, "You were just praying, and you don't know?" The other inmate responded, "Oh, I get it!" George quickly and boldly said to him, "No, you didn't get it!"

Now, within four months of his nineteenth birthday, George had done what he needed to do and it was so easy! George sincerely accepted Jesus Christ as his personal Savior that day. The bitterness was instantly removed. There was absolutely no more desire for drugs. In addition, even in prison, the stressed-out nervousness that produced the easily irritated rattlesnake instinct that was so tensely ready to strike was changed into a bunny rabbit-like temperament, so George would describe. Not that he couldn't or wouldn't bite, but he had really lost the fighting appetite.

Realistically George's thought process would not be fixed quickly. Anyone having a violent and abusive past such as his could only be fully changed over an extended period of time, but miraculously at least that day, George was relaxed and at peace. The nightmares ended, allowing a restful sleep for the first time in his memory. This was like experiencing a type of freedom in prison!

Those who have been incarcerated for any extended period can relate to the knots in the stomach common to prisoners. Until now they had stayed in George's stomach—they were now gone! Yes, he still had the potential to be dangerous and unpredictable, but he no longer really wanted to be! He knew deep down inside something had indeed changed. The rest of George's stay in that man-made hell as strange as this sounds was a little like heaven. And that Bible, he couldn't really read it to understand anything but it was the most comfortable pillow he could imagine ever having. He did not know how to witness, but he did. And even though no outside changes were visible yet, some inmates seemed to know something was different. So different that he quickly lost all his so-called friends.

Once on the way back from the chapel, three guys jumped him in part to provoke him to just go crazy as he used to do. They got a kick out of messing with heads; the games were kind of like a cross between a "shrinks" games to that of middle-school games. A favorite pastime was to be a show off of some kind.

For once in his life, he just took it, even looking one of them in the eye and saying, "Jesus loves you!" He then put a razor blade to George's throat. Yes, even in the hole, one could get such. George looked at him, smiling and said, "Go ahead, I will go to a better place!" Then they just let him go, walking off laughing, saying, "He's gone plumb crazy!" They had repeatedly punched him, knocked him down, and kicked him all over. George later realized he did not get a single bruise or scratch on him. The inmates would from then on have a very special place in his heart.

He wanted everyone to have what he had. It was better than the greatest high. He had peace in his heart and somehow that showed where it mattered most. In the last thirty days of his incarceration, he would have the pleasure of leading some into a sinner's prayer he had memorized from the chaplain. These included a rapist, a drug dealer, a thief, and a murderer. Those with no hope, which longed for it, could find it in Jesus! Moreover, they were not pretended relationships with Christ. In prison, if you claim to be a Christian, you could be teased or ridiculed as bad as the ones in check-in or protective custody! Christians were persecuted. Someone would often yell out things like, "How about turning the other cheek for me?" Not meaning the cheek on your face.

It was not George. He was just a con, quite like the others. This was the power of God! George could not explain it. It didn't even make sense to him. In all the time he was in there, he had only seen two or three who gave it up to God, and now within thirty days, to experience this great movement of God, the man who had put the blade to his throat was now a Christian, and he had a life sentence. This defined awesome to him. He now wanted to become a preacher, but he knew he had a lot to do before he could go there. With maybe, at best, a third-grade reading level, he began trying to teach himself to read the Bible.

Although this quickly appeared impossible, and the process was going to be especially difficult and much longer than his stay here in prison, the benefits from just finding the motivation to want to learn to read would be lifelong. This Bible is where he would learn about his God, as well as the many other changes he would now start undergoing. This is how the mind—the thinking—is changed. As if a whole new world began to be opened up to him, life itself had a new sense of adventure. The adventure of transformation into what God desired him to be would occupy his curiosity for a long time to come.

He spent most of his last day in prison reflecting on all that had taken place within those walls. It seemed as if he were there for years, not months. Realistically speaking, for one his age to be subjected to this kind of hard time would naturally impact and consume his thoughts, as if these months were actually years long. Actually between the ages of ten until this point, he had been confined to either a mental facility of some kind, a jail, and to prison. This was for over 20 percent of the years of his life. If you were forty and had just spent a few weeks of time in this place, it would have a dramatic embossing effect on the rest of your life. But to him, the drama that put him here was his life. He didn't really know how to or if he could even be different.

It was suddenly as if a spirit of fear clouded about him, he began to tremble in fear that he would return to the drugs. The streets had been his life. He was afraid and began quietly weeping. It was then that he remembered the words of one of his uncles; the one who was a Oneness Pentecostal. He had told him that he was guilty of blasphemy against the Holy Spirit, and that was an unforgivable sin, and he was surely going to hell! George was paralyzed by all of these thoughts.

Then it was as if God sent the chaplain to him at his darkest moment. He comes to see George one last time. He said he felt he needed to assure George that he was in fact now saved and a new creature. He assured George he had not committed the unpardonable sin, or he wouldn't even be concerned about it. He explained this is how Satan works. He comes to steal, kill, and destroy. He wanted him to know that he would be praying for him, to never be afraid of failing because he and other Christians would always have his back through prayer. Wow, George thought this guy was really connected to God. He had never said anything about what was on his mind, the chaplain just knew. He prayed with George again, and peace reigned and ruled again.

Finally the hour had arrived. He passes through the doors made of bars for the last time, then through the gate. He leaves those walls. The man-made hell called prison, with the number he had ripped off his shirt that had identified him for the past months. But he does so with a new attitude of hope and excitement in his newfound faith in God. This was just six weeks before his nineteenth birthday.

Closing Thoughts

The intent behind this book needs to be crystal clear. It is certainly not to glorify sin. There are few things a Christian can do worse than to make a sinful past seem so exciting that others would be attracted to it. This story is about exposing the effects of evil, the destruction, the pain, and the turmoil caused by such lifestyles. Then this story points toward a new and better life through The Lord, Jesus Christ.

The voids and out of context fragments of George's memory during periods of heavy drug use sent me on a search for information from those who knew him. Some incidents he said happened, others disbelieved happened. Some things others insisted happened, George would have no memory of, or was in disbelief that they even happened. A month to George, others said, was only a week, or what was said to be a week by George, others said was actually a month.

So in writing this story, I had to conclude that the true facts may never be known in this life. But one fact was for sure agreed upon by everyone who knew him before his release from prison: George was quite different now, and the change is credited to his new relationship with God. The God George was now beginning to follow is very real! He is the One True God, which we all assuredly will someday soon face. The question then becomes: "Are you ready?"

If this story has raised the questions: "Is it too late for me?" "Is there any hope for me?" "Can I even be saved?" Or if you're thinking, "If George could do it, so can I. But how?" Then please start by reading the following verses in the Bible, earnestly seeking to understand them:

John 3:16, Romans 3:23, Romans 6:23, Romans 5:8, Romans 10:9–10, Romans 10:13, Romans 10:23, 2 Corinthians 5:21, Romans 5:1, Romans 8:1, Romans 8:38–39.

In Romans 10:13 (NIV), "Everyone who calls on the name of the Lord will be saved."

This verse alone says that any person who will call upon the name of the Lord (Jesus) will be saved. First of all, understand this: to call means to earnestly ask in prayer. Then look at what the verse does not require. The verse does not require anyone to know anything else. It does not ask you to do better first. It puts no conditions on you cleaning up or changing your life first. Such would add to what the Bible says Jesus has already done for us on the cross.

George was still very much a thug-like person in the outward flesh. He didn't know how not to cuss or not to have bad thoughts, and he certainly did not know how to act like a respectable person. By God's grace through Jesus Christ, he was now a new creature *inside*.

Any outside changes you think you need to make or bad habits you feel you need to give up, do not need to happen before you're saved. After one is saved, as they grow in their faith by reading God's Word, they naturally will change their mind about this or that. As as the changes start to be applied, they will be through grace, not through condemnation. Rest assured in this, the price for salvation was fully paid on the cross by Christ and it was by His work, not by ours.

As a Christian, it is true that we are to each work out our own soul's salvation. However, Christians are to do this, not sinners! We do this day by day, not all at once. As we walk in the truth of how He walked before us, and as we grow closer to Him, we will become more like Him. So you need not change anything in your life before you are saved. Perhaps you also need to understand that after you're truly saved, you will begin to have a different thinking as you learn of His ways. What you don't want to give up now or are afraid you can't give up, will change into something you want to give up, and you will find a strength you cannot imagine now. George was delivered, instantly of many addictive things, yet worked his way through others. We all have individual needs and issues, yet God knows and addresses each of our needs differently as individuals, yet always with the same unconditional love and seemingly endless patience toward us all.

If you don't personally have an ongoing relationship with Jesus Christ, then He is not the Lord of your life. We all serve a god, but not necessarily The One True God! Many people follow false gods or simply choose to serve themselves as if they were a god. Know this, after this life is gone, there is a time approaching where every knee will bow to The God of the Holy Bible. This day will be very traumatic for all those who neglect to bow to Him in this life. Many are deceived, believing they are Christian's under false doctrines, or by believing they are saved merely based on the fact that they believe in God. Don't you realize that even Satan believes in God and knows Him better than we do? Satan's destiny is Hell! The decision about his future has already been made, and he wants you to join him in Hell for eternity. There is some great news. You do have a choice. If you would like to avoid Hell, you must make the choice to make

Jesus the Lord of your life, you must be born again. To experience this rebirth, receive Jesus as your personal Savior. Pray this prayer, believing it in your heart as you pray it:

> Dear Heavenly Father, I come to you in the name of Jesus, believing that He is Your only begotten Son, and that He shed His blood on Calvary as a price for my sins. I acknowledge to You that I am a sinner, and that I am sorry for my sins, and for the way I have lived my life. I am now willing to turn from my sins and follow Your ways. I believe what Your Word says in Romans 10:9, and right now, I confess Jesus as the Lord of my soul. With my heart, I believe that You raised Jesus from the dead, and at this moment I accept Jesus Christ as my personal Savior, and believing according to Your Word that I am now a new creature. I am now born again. I am saved. Thank you Jesus, Amen.

If you earnestly prayed this prayer believing it, then you are saved. Welcome to the family of God. Now go and tell someone, don't bottle it up. Find a Bible-believing church as soon as possible and begin fellowshipping with other Christians as much as you can. Get baptized as soon as possible to outwardly expose the fact to others that the old person is dead and a new one has arisen. Get into God's Word—the Bible—and learn what His will is for your life. Get involved in a structured study with other believers searching for understanding. Pray for an empowerment of the Holy Spirit that you can gain the *power* to resist temptation and to be a witness for Christ.

Perhaps you were baptized in the past or as a small child—brother or sister—although there is no case mentioned in the Bible of an individual being baptized more than once, there is nothing in the Bible saying you can't do it again. I know this will open some cans of religious worms regarding once saved always saved versus backsliding; and submersion versus sprinkling. Those who have been back to the water after living a sinful lifestyle and have come up out of the water, have often testified that the benefits of another water baptism is immeasurable. Just saying!

Perhaps you're in or have been in an abusive relationship, or you're emotionally scarred from a past trauma, or maybe you yourself are or have been abusive, or you're caught up in some kind of addiction. I have good news: First of all, there is a God who is here to help you. You can be miraculously delivered; sometimes some things instantly, other times over time. Often deliverance comes through the help of others. One of the tools He uses are counselors. There are many reputable godly Christian counselors available.

In this story, there were situations that displayed poor counseling, or the lack of wise counseling. However, often professional counseling is very much needed. This story was not intended to detour anyone from getting needed counseling, but rather highlight the need for wise counseling. This book also displayed a negative side to prescription drugs. This was not to say that there are not times and uses for them. The Bible instructs us to seek wise counsel, to avoid leaning on our own understanding. The need for wise counseling is beneficial in circumstances about everyday life, but it is especially crucial toward overcoming such traumatic things as experienced by George.

A description of a biblical wise counselor would be a man or woman of God, (being found faithful themselves) who possess a time-proven dedication toward understanding and applying the will of God toward resolving the issues of life. No one pastor or psychologist possesses such regarding every aspect of everyone's life. This is part of the reason the Bible says that in the multitude of counselors there is safety.

Often in such situations as George went through, a Christian psychologist, more often than not, would be far better equipped to assist one through some of the more complex things better than most any pastor. Ministers of the Gospel need to invest time in prayer and study, for the overall edification of the believers, not just be consumed with the mental issues or drama of each person. If each person dumped all their garbage on them they would have no time to even read the Scriptures. Seek wise counseling, just seek it! The key thing is in searching for wise counsel through biblical principles, not through man's reasoning, and especially not through your own intellect.

This country's prisons are full of common people, men and women alike, who simply chose to work a situation out their own way, or by the way of ill-guided advice from others. History has long shown that the lack of wisdom fills jails and prisons, and the lack of it will cause many to return to it more than just once. Many of which are mothers and fathers themselves. What about their families?

It also cannot go without saying that our jails and prisons have many war heroes. It's been said that 30 percent of veterans of the United States Armed Forces, have come back from battle with PTSD, and many were left to treat themselves by the way of drugs and alcohol, resulting in criminal behavior. Sadly, it's been noted that many come back from war already with like addictions. And our government has turned its back on many of them. Then when they commit crimes, no one will accept that they are a victim too.

If you're currently incarcerated and realize you need counseling, you should be able to get it! You have some basic rights that are still protected under the US Constitution. Such includes entitlement and access to mental health care, and such treatment must also be adequate. But above all seek spiritual counsel with the chaplain. Think about it, the chaplain is certainly not there because it's just a job, they have that job because they want to help you. You matter!

A common simplified testimony of Christians is this: "I once was lost and now I'm found." George could never leave it quite that simple. He once was lost, and then he found a road map. In book 2, *Entangled*, you will quickly see that his inability to read and understand that map required wise counseling; Godly guidance that he didn't want or believe that he even needed. Although without such guidance, he experiences God's mercy and grace like as if it were the manna from heaven that fell upon the Israelites. Like them, he also begins dwelling in a desolate wilderness for some time due to his own thinking, before he finally realizes this and starts the quest for wisdom through godly counseling.

If you are a Christian and this story has moved you, and you believe this story should go forth, then pass your copy along or even get a few more copies to share, or just tell others about it. Post it on your blogs or on your social media sites. If you purchased your copy online, go back to that site and post a reader's review.

My goal for this work is that multiple copies of book 1 *Mangled* be placed into every prison library in the United States. Then to provide literally every county jail in every state at least a copy. Then to every city jail for inmates to pass around. In addition, for book 2 *Entangled!* and *book 3 Intertwined!* to become published as preventive tools. Thus cutting down on like evils in our future generations. Then to stand in prayer letting God and time judge the rest. I am but a single ant, I cannot do this alone, but together we can take our nation back—one heart at a time! Will you try with me?

I am sure of this, if we don't immediately make a firm decision to act united as one, this once great nation is in line for God's wrath, much like Sodom and Gomorrah. Christians today who choose to hold fast to sound biblical views are facing persecution, and we will soon be jailed for standing for truth. Some say, "Well, it's the End Times. We all knew it would come to an end." But I tell you, it will end even sooner if we do nothing! Do you really think we will be judged innocently by doing nothing? I would hope not!

Back in 2012, a ten-year study was concluded by the US Justice Department on nonfatal domestic violence, attributing that well over 20 percent of all violent victimizations to be domestic in nature. Domestic violence includes rape, sexual assault, robbery, and aggravated and simple assault, committed by intimate partners, immediate family members, or other relatives. or casual acquaintances accounted for well over 30 percent of all violent victimizations.

This study indicated that out of an average of nearly seven million annually reported cases of abuse, only 38 percent were actually committed by total strangers. Then there is another well-known fact that should be factored in, and that is many cases of abuse among family members goes totally unreported to the authorities. This not only magnifies the actual cases of abuse by those we know and trust but also is sound evidence indicating that we really do hurt the ones we love! There is often a diagnosable or explainable underlying issue behind much of this abuse, and many forms of treatment are available. If we would just open up to wisdom, we could at a minimum, cut back on the future cases of needless pain!

Now here is some more statistical insight that I find shocking: over 240 cases of child abuse are reported a day, in New York City alone. How many cases are there where you live? Better yet, what are you doing about it? Are you just minding your own business?

As of August 2015, there were 3,143 county-equivalents in the United States, some counties have multiple county jails as well as several city jails; having some twenty thousand jails of some kind in the United States. There is an incalculable number of people arrested and processed through from those who only stay a few hours or for a few days. To those who will be sentenced to serve a term, there is currently nearly four hundred thousand men, women, and youth serving an extend sentence to a prison or detention center.

On this date, there are 4,575 prisons in the USA. We have more than any other country in the world. Russia is in second place with 1,029 prisons. Incarcerations are on the rise while Christian's involvement in works of prevention is on the decline. Why? Could it be because we boast that our ticket to heaven is not by works, lest any man boast? As a result, many of us have forgotten our duty to do the work of visiting those who are imprisoned. Many of us, in times past, have done many of the very things others were convicted of, and are jailed for, while we walk free. If this is you, and you haven't done some righteous works regarding this, here's your chance.

Partner with me regarding this. After you have finished reading your copy, simply drop it off at your local city or county jail for the inmates to read. Or better yet, for every crime you have secretly committed or have not paid a debt to society for yourself, I challenge you to purchase a Bible and personally hand it with your copy of this book to an inmate somewhere. Talk about a field of ministering possibilities. Our jails house many who have so much idle time that reading books like the Bible or this book is but a way of passing time. Pass this to them, and pray some, open their hearts; and when they are released back into society, our country will have become a better place—one soul at a time.

CPSIA information can be obtained
at www.ICGtesting.com
Printed in the USA
FSOW04n1547290716
23235FS

9 781683 333715